As an avid reader through the decades, I have found precious few books given to the subject of Joseph of Nazareth. We are blessed to have this new volume by Fran Riedemann. To write historical fiction requires endless research and insight, which the author most certainly gives us in this new work. Far from being rampant speculation, Fran has revealed to us an authentic look at the man God entrusted to raise His earthly Son. I thoroughly enjoy a book of this nature which "fleshes out scripture" where we are often left looking for more information. You will have a grand time with this volume you now hold in your hands.

—Dan Betzer, Sr. Pastor,
First Assembly Ministries, Ft. Myers, Fl.

A poignant, touching story that reveals the vital and important role of a strong, committed father in a family. Riedemann's tale should inspire all men to love and serve their wives, sons and daughters as the true fathers God has called them to be.

—Mark Gungor, Laugh Your Way
to a Better Marriage Seminars

God chose Joseph for one of the most important missions in history—to be a father to Jesus on earth. And yet we know so little about him. Fran Riedemann weaves a story to help us know this extraordinary man.

—Wendy Wright, President of
Concerned Women for America

I have met Fran Riedemann on a couple of occasions; she is one of the faithful in Him.

Joseph was used because he was listening for God to speak to him and recognized His voice when he did. What a blessing to have the opportunity to discover some of the attributes that set him apart for God to be used in such a profound way.

—Director/ Pastor Karen Dunham
Living Bread International Church

Rarely does one stop to think about what kind of an earthly father Jesus must have had. In this book we catch a glimpse of what Joseph set aside in order to become the earthly father of the Messiah. Riedemann's imaginative and insightful presentation of Joseph is thought–provoking and enjoyable reading. She causes us to think about the role of fathers in our culture today and the huge impact they have on the lives of their families.

—Kenda Bartlett, National Field Director
of Concerned Women for America

Biblical fatherhood is well taught in Scripture and is foundational to so much of life, touching us all in some way. I personally had a wonderful dad and my experiences were overwhelmingly positive. For others, a father relationship often doesn't exist; resulting in the dysfunctional father syndrome being perpetuated. Rescue Missions like City Union Mission see this everyday in the men and women who, unfortunately, are only practicing what they were taught.

In *Joseph: the heart of the father*, Fran tells a refreshing and enlightening story of Biblical fatherhood–what a father whose walk is focused on God can be or become.

—Rev. Daniel J. Doty, Executive Director
City Union Mission, Kansas City, Missouri

Reading this book gave me an opportunity to reflect upon the role of fathers. What my own father did to give me a better life influenced its course. What a privileged role a father has; to be able to guide, encourage, correct, protect, and to bless their children. Enjoy this rare opportunity to be able to look more closely at the character of Joseph and ponder the connection he shared with the Heavenly Father.

—Hélène Pelletier, Radio & Television journalist, Reseau Des Sports, Quebec, Canada

JOSEPH

JOSEPH
THE HEART OF THE FATHER

FRAN RIEDEMANN

Tate Publishing & Enterprises

Published by Tate Publishing & Enterprises, LLC
127 E. Trade Center Terrace | Mustang, Oklahoma 73064 USA
1.888.361.9473 | www.tatepublishing.com

Tate Publishing is committed to excellence in the publishing industry. The company reflects the philosophy established by the founders, based on Psalm 68:11,
"The Lord gave the word and great was the company of those who published it."

Book design copyright © 2010 by Tate Publishing, LLC. All rights reserved.
Cover design by Kellie Southerland
Interior design by Lindsay B. Behrens

Published in the United States of America

ISBN: 978-1-61566-807-6
1. Religion / Christianity / History   2. Fiction / Christian / Historical
10.01.19

ACKNOWLEDGEMENTS

I want to thank my husband who has been my life's partner and best encourager. Kenneth Riedemann has always pushed me to do what I didn't think I was equipped or capable of doing and he has held my hand through the failures and successes that make up the pursuit of reaching the higher ground.

My sister–in–law, Phyllis Griffith, was the first person to anoint my book with her tears. She immediately embraced the characters and the message of the story. She and my friend, Irvilene Gardner, have read and reread my manuscript countless times and prayed me to this end. I am in debt to them both.

There are the unexpected confirmations that give our dreams wings as we go along. My deepest thanks goes to Pastor Connie Weisel who distinguished this work by reading it, recommending it, and embracing what the Spirit was saying through it. Her belief in the book, and in me, is a priceless gift.

I also thank my encouragers; Patty Harvey, Cuky Harvey, Ann Sicilia, Jenanne Jenkins, and Susan Cousins who believed in the book long before it was one. A special thanks to Rev. Rob Winger who read the manuscript in the beginning and shared his thoughts and insights with me.

How does one put into words the reality of the amazing presence and wisdom of the Holy Spirit who whispers words to us that we could never have thought of ourselves? Without Him there would be no story.

I dedicate this to the memory of my father,
Robert R. Ernst

TABLE OF CONTENTS

FOREWORD

by Pastor Connie Weisel

I have always loved to read. I fondly remember growing up in our old centennial farmhouse in Southwest Ohio where we had large window seats. They were perfect for hiding away with a good book. Since then I've read books in many, many places. I don't remember most of those places. I don't even remember most of the books. But a few—a precious few—seem as vivid to me now as the day I first read them. And so it is with this book.

I met Fran Riedemann during a trying time in her life. She was looking for a listening heart,

Godly wisdom, and encouragement. I hope she found some of that in my office that day. I know what I found, or I guess it found me, as she handed me the transcript of the book you now hold, and casually asked me to "please read it when I had time." I toted it around in my briefcase for months. I was intrigued by the concept: a book about Jesus's earthly father. It captured my imagination immediately, but it took a while before it captured my time. Once I began to read, my heart was captured as well.

In the late 70s, I traveled to Sweden for a large Robotics Show and Symposium. My husband, Walt, was President of the Robotics Industries Association at the time and acted as host during the show to the King of Sweden, King Carl XVI Gustaf. He was a very congenial man. Professionally, he was interested in modern technology, especially robotics. But he was also personally interested in my husband, and for a most unusual reason! At the time, I looked and acted very much like his new wife, Silvia, of German and Brazilian descent. As Walt introduced me to the King, I was of special interest to him because I reminded him so much of her. It kind of worked like this … The King wanted to know if those attributes that had drawn my husband to me were the same as those that had drawn him to his beloved Silvia. He met her in 1972 at the Summer Olympics in Munich, were she served as an interpreter and host. He wanted to know my husband more, in order to know more about me, through him. Interesting …

And yet, you know how this works. You want to get to know somebody better because they're close to somebody you want to know better. That's just what this book did to me. I found myself wanting to know Joseph better … his thoughts, his struggles, his choices, his heart … as he raised Jesus in those early formative years.

Even though much of it is fiction, somehow I am certain it's more than that. It's a gift from our Heavenly Father to help us know the Son even more as He is seen through the eyes of His earthly father. As we know Joseph more, we somehow know Jesus more. How wonderful!

I recently got online and, interestingly enough, the Queen and I still somewhat favor one another. That really doesn't matter at all. What does matter is that you hold one of those precious few books in your hands. So do yourself a favor. Go find your own window seat and hide away with this book. I'm pretty sure you'll remember it for a very long time.

MATTHEW 1: 18–25

This is how Jesus the Messiah was born. His mother, Mary, was engaged to be married to Joseph. But before her marriage took place, while she was still a virgin, she became pregnant through the power of the Holy Spirit. Joseph, her fiancé, was a good man and did not want to disgrace her publicly, so he decided to break the engagement quietly.

As he considered this, an angel of the Lord appeared to him in a dream. "Joseph, son of David," the angel said, "do not be afraid to take Mary as your wife. For the child within her was conceived by the Holy Spirit. And she will have a son, and you are to name him Jesus, for he will save his people from their sins."

All of this occurred to fulfill the Lord's message through the prophet: Look a virgin will conceive a child! She will give birth to a son. And they will call him Immanuel, which means 'God is with us'. When Joseph woke up, he did as the angel of the Lord commanded and took Mary as his wife. But he did not have sexual relations with her until her son was born.

And Joseph named him Jesus.

PROLOGUE

The weary couple leaned against the stone wall outside the temple courtyard. They glanced around nervously, speaking to each other in low tones about what to do next. Dirty and disheveled, they were completely taken aback by the large numbers of people milling around them; other Jewish pilgrims who had stayed behind after the Passover. They were taking every precaution to remain as inconspicuous as possible, feeling very vulnerable.

After three days of frantic searching throughout Jerusalem, they had received word that their missing boy might be here. Now they asked themselves why they hadn't come here first. Cautiously they pressed through the jumble of people and into the Temple's outer courtyard.

Joseph of Nazareth tightened his grip around his wife's waist hoping to ease her trembling and, by doing so, he steadied himself as well.

He could read her thoughts, for they were his own.

They were standing but a few feet from where the old man Simeon had noticed them twelve years earlier when they brought their baby boy to the temple to be circumcised and given his name; where the elderly man had announced he could die in peace because he had at last seen the promised Messiah.

The confirmation of their child's destiny spoken through him could not dispel the uneasiness his words produced in his mother, Mary, when he suddenly reached out and took the baby right out of her arms, proclaiming loudly to whoever was nearby: "Sovereign Lord, now let your servant die in peace, as you have promised. I have seen your salvation, which you have prepared for all people. He is a light to reveal God to the nations, and He is the glory of your people, Israel."

Alarmed, the new mother looked at her husband; she was overwhelmed to think it was possible for them to be exposed like this, without any warning. Joseph reacted instinctively by firmly but gently extricating the baby from the arms of the old man, returning him to his wife.

Her discomfort at their being recognized was not without good reasons. The extraordinary circumstances of the infant's birth just eight days earlier, accompanied by the unexpected visit by the shepherds to his birthplace, caused them both to realize their vulnerability in being pointed out.

Joseph attempted to explain his concern to Simeon, but the old man was now fixated on the young mother, offering a blessing over her and Joseph.

Undeterred, he proceeded to prophesy over their baby. "This child is destined to cause many in Israel to fall, but He will be a joy to many others. He has been sent as a sign from God, but many will oppose him. As a result, the deepest thoughts of many hearts will be revealed. And a sword will pierce your very soul."

Mary stepped backwards, putting distance between her and the well–intended, but unwelcomed, intruder.

Joseph thanked him; he was aware this moment was significant to Simeon as well as to them, but he was determined to escape from him. He took Mary by the elbow and quickly steered her in another direction, away from the old man with the intention of diverting his wife's attention back to the purpose for them being there.

No more had they moved away from Simeon than an old woman named Anna spotted them and hobbled their way boasting that this was the child sent who would be the rescuer of Jerusalem.

With or without their permission, their child's destiny was confirmed to them on the steps of the Temple.

The boy was indeed their son.

He looked remarkable because of his simplicity and his young age. That he was from no impressive social status was obvious. His robe had been woven from the coarsest linen and was threadbare and mended; his sandals patched and worn. Yet, amazingly, he sat surrounded by the elders and leaders of the Sanhedrin, who were leaning toward him and listening intently to his comments regarding their inquiries, marveling at the quality of the answers he threw back at them. After each topic was thoroughly debated a new round discussion was introduced by the older men to their unlikely colleague

The boy named Jesus was seated in the place of honor, centered by a semi–circle of religious teachers where an honored guest might have been asked to sit. He appeared calm, his hands were folded in his lap; his expression was intense, eager, showing his enjoyment to be included in the discussions. He also leaned forward in his eagerness to discover what the next topic might be. His demeanor showed that he felt no unease in this unique setting and was thoroughly enjoying this interval of energetic debate.

Indeed, it was a most unusual sight.

Joseph returned to Jerusalem each spring for Passover, bringing along his family who were joined by other relatives and friends who all looked forward to the yearly reunion. For Mary, each visit inevitably evoked a flood of conflicted emotions. She had so many unanswered questions that were revived by events like these. Much of the time she was able to pretend that she and Joseph were a normal family; their daily lives were so ordinary. But, at moments like these, she would feel the viselike grip that tightened around her heart when she remembered the unusual beginnings of Joseph's and her life together.

Whatever their son's destiny, it was dangerous for him to be exposed like this. The rumors of a rescuer who would incite a rebellion against Rome were continually floating in the wind. Many of them were spread with deliberate seditious intent on the part of the Romans, targeting the Jewish people. Ironically, the more extreme rumors circulated within the communities of Jews, brought about by their frustration in being squeezed ever tighter by the Romans; reeling under the imposition of burdensome taxes and the ongoing restrictions of their liberties.

Their desperate longing to see an end to Roman tyranny made them vulnerable to any thread of hope that was dangled in front of them. They longed for a leader who could rescue them, and a faction believed in a messiah who when revealed would deliver them by force. Were their son to become associated with any part of the ever–evolving rumors, the consequences could be deadly … for them all.

The outlines of crosses punctuated the land-scape; blatant public displays of anyone even rumored to be a dissident. The Romans took no chances with civil disobedience, even implied, relishing any opportunity to make an example of such behavior by way of their barbaric cru-elty, particularly if one was a Jew. There were still other sects who were in conflict with each other, notwithstanding the eldership who were now intently questioning their son.

Mary abruptly shook off Joseph's protective hand and stepped in front of him before he could stop her. They had finally managed to edge their way to the front of the crowd, although they were unnoticed by Jesus. All she wanted to do was to get their boy out of there and go home to the safety of Nazareth.

"Jesus!" she cried, "We have been frantically trying to find you! Your father and I have been searching for you for days!"

The boy registered no surprise at her sharp reproof, but simply said, "Mother, you had no need to look for me. Didn't you know I must be about my Father's business?"

Mary turned abruptly toward her husband. She gave Joseph a hard look, wondering what business matter he could have discussed with their son to have caused this near calamity, putting them through the anguish of the last few days.

But Joseph's eyes had focused somewhere else; somewhere far beyond the present moment. He sensed in his spirit that God was confirming what he had known for some time; that his time with Jesus would soon be drawing to a close. He knew it would be necessary for him to step aside; he had always known there was but one Father who could accompany Jesus on the remainder of the journey. Joseph sighed deeply, bringing his attention back to the events that were occurring around him.

Jesus rose to his feet. He spoke politely to the seated elders, bowing respectfully to each one. He turned to join his parents who were already pushing their way back through the crowd, eager to be outside the Temple grounds and back on the street.

The three quickly disappeared into the crowd before anyone could inquire about who they were.

CHAPTER ONE

With exaggerated emphasis, Joseph pounded the final leg into the stool he was making; the last one to a set of four. He turned it over and held it up so he could admire it for a moment. It represented the near completion of his labor of love for his betrothed wife, Mary.

He set it on the floor and smiled to himself, tossing his hammer aside and stretching his arms over his head to ease the stiffness in his neck and shoulders. He allowed himself the luxury of a groan while he rolled his head from side to side, relieved to be finished for the day.

He stood to his feet and untied the apron he wore while he worked. Stepping outside he shook it off and hung it on a peg by the door. He went back inside and gathered up his tools, arranging them neatly in a crate he kept in the corner.

Turning around, he appreciatively took in the details of the little house. The satisfaction of a job well done caused him to smile again. He had never known such happiness. It was dusk, and only the darkening sky kept him from working far into the night, making everything perfect.

The betrothal period that was required before they could marry was nearly over. Any day now Mary would be returning home from visiting her cousin Elizabeth, and their marriage could be finalized.

He couldn't help but anticipate her reaction when he showed her the house and the furnishings he had been preparing for them to begin their married life. It had been several months since he had seen her; the passage of time feeling like an eternity to him. His consolation was that he had been able to devote himself to having everything ready for her when she returned home. There was nothing else that stood in the way of their being married immediately.

Tomorrow at sundown the Sabbath would begin. *Ah, a day of rest would be welcome!* Joseph repented his total preoccupation in working on their house and that he had to be compelled to lay aside his sense of urgency for even one day to reflect on his many blessings from the Lord. He had prayed a lifetime about who would become his wife never dreaming it possible that he would one day marry someone as completely lovely as Mary. He still had trouble believing it was true.

His sister, Ruth, would no doubt be annoyed with him once again. His immersion in his task had resulted in his losing track of time, seemingly disregarding her generous invitation to join her family for supper; by now they would already be eating. He did appreciate her making room for him at their table. Watching his brother–in–law, Judas, with his sister and the antics of their lively family made Joseph even more anxious to have one of his own.

Tomorrow he would apologize. Ruth adored her big brother, and she was delighted that he had finally become betrothed and that she would soon have a sister. Her forgiving him would not be an issue.

He decided to walk off the tension that had been building up inside him; tonight would be a good night to fast and pray, and to ask God to bless his future with his new bride.

He located the pouch that contained the prayer shawl that had once belonged to his father. It was his most valued possession; the mantle of his own father's unconditional love. His examples of Godly conduct were renewed whenever Joseph drew it over his head and called to remembrance God's promises that had been taught to him throughout his life by his father who had understood the loving–kindness of God as shown in His everlasting Covenants.

Joseph headed out, grateful for the chill that settled quickly once the sun retreated behind the hilly landscape. Drawing in deep, cleansing breaths of the cool night air, he began his hike up the rocky slopes, looking up to see stars already illuminating the darkening sky.

He climbed the same path he and his father had taken when Joseph was a boy. He could feel his tension easing while he climbed up the familiar hillside; he began singing one of David's psalms.

Many of Joseph's deeper lessons about God and His Covenants with His people had come during those times of solitude with his father, whose wisdom had been a deep well, continually refreshed by waiting on God. As time went by Joseph became more and more grateful for the priceless heritage of his father's determination to know God and to teach his sons to do the same.

His father had passed along to Joseph and his brothers his trade of carpentry, along with his examples of kindness, generosity, and honesty, but his true legacy was having instilled in his children his unwavering trust in God's faithfulness to His people as taught throughout the scriptures.

Joseph looked down at his hands, turning them over and noting that they now exhibited the patina of his occupation. Likewise, his father's hands had been rough and calloused, but oh so gentle when placed on his children's heads to bless them throughout their lives; his perfume was the smell of wood and earth that clung to his clothing and beard.

Joseph longed for the day he and Mary would be blessed with children, children they would instruct in the rich heritage of being Jewish by tradition and example. The father's honored role in his family was to pass on that legacy to yet another generation, teaching them to observe all the things the Lord God had commanded and to look forward to God's promise to redeem his people.

When Joseph reached the familiar plateau, he slipped out of his outer robe, spreading it out on the stony ground. He removed his prayer shawl from its pouch, recalling his father's pride the day he had placed it on Joseph's head when he had come of age. Joseph ran his hands over it. One day he hoped it would be worn by his own son. The thought brought another smile.

Joseph dropped to his knees, reciting the words of King David, "I rejoice in your word like one who discovers great treasure. I hate and abhor all falsehood, but I love your instructions."

He repented of his own sins of commission and omission, raising his hands toward the heavens. "Yes, I obey your commandments and laws, because you know everything I do. Oh Lord, listen as I praise you seven times a day because all your regulations are just. Those who love your instructions have great peace and do not stumble. I long for your rescue, Lord, so I have obeyed your commands. I have obeyed your laws, for I love them very much; give me the discerning mind you promised. Listen to my prayer; rescue me as you promised. Let praise flow from my lips, for you have taught me your decrees. Let my tongue sing about your word, for all your commands are right. Give me a helping hand, for I have chosen to follow your commandments."

A shooting star streaked across the sky, catching his eye; the sky was now alive with multitudes of sparkling stars. Joseph reminded God of His Covenant to Abraham, that He would "multiply his descendants beyond number, like the stars in the sky." God had told him that all the families would be blessed through him. He was righteous in God's eyes because he believed Him. Joseph's heart's desire was to know God in that way. If he was the last man standing he hoped his faith would bring him to the place where he could say what Job said, "But as for me, I know that my Redeemer lives, and that he will stand upon the earth at last. And after my body has decayed, yet in my body will I see God. I will see Him for myself. Yes, I will see Him with my own eyes. I am overwhelmed at the thought." Yes, Joseph's heart's desire was to be overwhelmed by God.

Many of his kinsmen no longer believed in the promise of a redeemer, but when Joseph recalled the God's Covenant He made with Abraham his own faith became refreshed again; he knew that God would one day fulfill every promise He had made to the people He had set apart for Himself.

Joseph lay on the ground on top of his robe. It had been four hundred years since God had spoken to them through the prophet Malachi. Many Jews no longer believed in a messiah, but there was still a remnant that looked for the one promised to come and relieve their oppression.

Joseph feared the price would be their own blood were his kinsmen to get the kind of leader they were asking for. Joseph believed that the redeemer would come to change their hearts first. The Jews were a stubborn and rebellious people; Joseph cried out to the Lord in their behalf. Only by obedience to God and His law given to Moses would they ever dwell in safety. They had all but forgotten His mighty works in their behalf.

Create in your people clean hearts, Oh Lord and Rock of our Salvation.

Yes, God would again reveal himself to His people. Perhaps it would happen in his lifetime. One family, one day, would be called upon to fulfill the prophecies that began with God's Word to Eve, that a woman would one day bear a child who would crush the head of the evil one. One day the curse on mankind would be lifted.

God was true to His word. His promises were eternal. Joseph called on the God of Covenant to once again reveal Himself to the people He called "the apple of his eye."

CHAPTER TWO

Joseph was uncomfortably crouched in a corner in the house he had been building for Mary. The stool he had made just days before was now broken and strewn in pieces across the floor, his tools in disarray. Large pock marks mocked him from the plastered walls where the tools had struck before they fell to the floor; his anger now giving way to the utter despair that was closing in on him was telling his world was falling apart.

He had known his feelings for Mary were strong, but up until this very moment he had not fully comprehended that he loved her beyond logic. The thought of losing her was too much for him to bear. His face dropped to his knees, huge racking sobs tore at him from within; grief and anger pouring out while he wordlessly offered God the crushing loss of his dreams and future.

Thoughts about her barraged him. *What could she be thinking? What had she done? What would they do to her? How could this have happened?*

He couldn't begin to imagine what the aftermath might be for Mary or for her family.

His sister had taken him aside when he arrived at her home that evening for supper asking him if he was aware that Mary had returned.

Ruth's stern demeanor troubled him. *Had she been crying?* Her hands shot out, grabbing both his arms and gripping them tightly. Her voice trembled with emotion. "Joseph, have you seen Mary since she returned home?"

Joseph shook his head, aware of a tightening in his abdomen.

Ruth's fingernails dug through his robe into his arms. She closed her eyes, taking several deep breaths before speaking again. "Joseph, I am too angry to discuss this right now, but I deserve to know what you and Mary are planning to do about her condition."

Joseph stepped back, not believing what his sister was inferring. "Condition?" he asked, his voice a hoarse whisper.

Ruth looked intently into Joseph's eyes. "*The child, Joseph!* How could you have brought this shame on our family, or on Mary's?"

A moan escaped from Joseph; roughly he shoved Ruth away from him.

She released him, startled as she tried to catch herself before falling backward. His reaction seemed as though he truly had not known, although that seemed impossible. She could not imagine sitting across from him at supper tonight, and it was just as well that he knew why.

But that was no longer a problem. Joseph was gone.

When Ruth learned that Mary had returned home she was beside herself with anticipation. Being the only girl in her family she was delighted to at last have a sister to share things with. On her way to the well that morning she deliberately walked out of her way, going by Mary's father's house, hoping to see her.

While Ruth was still a few houses away Mary emerged, picked up something from off the ground, turned and went back inside, unaware that she had been observed. Ruth couldn't believe her eyes. *Could she be with child?*

Ruth was devastated, thinking ahead to the gossip that would sweep through Nazareth at the discovery. *How would she ever explain this to her children?*

Confused and angry she turned back, unsure what one was supposed to do when confronted with something this catastrophic.

No, she had to be sure! She backtracked, concealing herself behind a wall a few houses from their house. She had to know for sure before she confronted Joseph. Perhaps she was wrong. She desperately wanted to be wrong.

After a long wait, Mary again stepped outside.

There was no mistake.

She seethed with rage. *When was the girl going to tell Joseph, or was it possible he already knew?* No wonder she had gone away to stay at her cousin's! The question she was asking herself was, *Why had she come back now, or at all?*

Surely Mary would have to know there would be consequences; and the consequences could be deadly.

J oseph remained uncomfortably slumped in the corner of the room holding his head in his hands. He pressed his temples with his fingertips as if some miraculous discernment might be expressed if he squeezed his head hard enough. *Oh, Mary, Mary, what am I to do? What can I do? Oh, God, help me!*

He knew it would only be a short time before someone would make it their business to inform the elders of their synagogue that Mary was with child. If the charge brought against her proved to be true, her fate would be determined according to Moses's Law. The Law was clear. Mary would be stoned.

Nothing like this had ever happened in Nazareth in Joseph's lifetime. Presuming they believed that it was his child, he was uncertain what might happen to him as well. Both of their lives were inextricably damaged. He immediately reminded himself of the Word of the Lord: "*My heart is confident in you, Oh God.*" It seemed impossible, but he sensed God with him even in the midst of his despair.

He knew that he could not let her die. Tomorrow he would go to her father as he had planned, only instead of planning for a marriage, they would arrange for a private divorce. Her father could send her away: perhaps Elizabeth would again help her. It would be a disgrace for her family, but her life and the child's would be spared. He could worry about himself later.

Having come to some conclusions gave him a degree of comfort as twilight faded into night. His eyes burned within their sockets and his chest hurt, but finally he fell into a restless sleep.

A shaft of pure white light slanted across his slumped figure, shining down on him through a small window high in the wall opposite from where he slept. When he awoke, the full revelation of his years of searching the scriptures and crying out to God to speak to his people again had become his new reality. The angel said, "Joseph, do not be afraid to take Mary to be your wife, for the child within her was conceived by the Holy Spirit. She shall have a son, and you are to name him Jesus, for He shall save his people from their sins."

The light continued streaming into the room, blanketing him with a peculiar sense of peace.

Every abstract thought and pondering of his entire lifetime had crystallized, the words of the scriptures springing to life within Him. Yes, God would again visit his people. The people would have their redeemer.

He must go to Mary and tell her everything was going to be okay! Mary was carrying Israel's hope within her. It was the will of Jehovah that Joseph be their protector.

At first light Joseph went outside to watch the sun rise. It was as if the light was penetrating into his very core. *My heart is confident in you, O God; no wonder I can sing your praises with all my heart.*

The song of a warbler broke the silence, calling the little village to begin its day.

Joseph went inside to straighten up the mess he had made the night before. He was prepared to go to his betrothed.

Shouldn't he feel exhausted? Instead he felt renewed, revived, despite the hugeness of what God was asking of him.

The angel's words were confirmation of precisely what God had been showing him in the scriptures regarding the Messiah that was to come; the fulfillment of what the Lord had spoken by the prophet, Isaiah: 'Behold the virgin shall conceive and bear a son, and His name shall be called Immanuel; God with us'.

The "revolt" would not be liberation from their oppressors, but instead they would be emancipated from their disobedience and the bondage of the Law.

Joseph knew they had been given a daunting mission, but he rested in the One who would help them accomplish it.

Hidden behind the same low wall where Ruth had waited the day before, Joseph waited for Mary to appear, rehearsing what to say to her.

At last she stepped through the doorway, pulling her shawl around her, concealing her waistline. She reached down and picked up a clay jar that was leaning against the house and began walking toward him. It was not his intention to startle her, but there was no way to avoid it; he had to seize the moment.

He stepped out where she could see him. She was deep in thought; her preoccupation causing her to be distracted. She looked up to see Joseph standing a few yards in front of her. She stopped, the moment frozen in time for both of them. They stared at each other for what seemed like an eternity, neither knowing what to say. Joseph spoke first, "Mary..." The jug dropped to the earth with a thud when she cast it aside to run to him.

Then the words tumbled out of him. "Mary, I know about the angel's visit to you; I know about the baby. We must be married right away. The LORD will show us what to do."

Mary looked into Joseph's eyes registering no surprise, but listening calmly while he declared his commitment to her and to the child she was carrying. Joseph recognized the courage of the small woman he would soon marry, and her faith that God would protect and keep her from harm. It dawned on him how unwavering her faith had to be for her to have returned to Nazareth to face him and disclose her situation.

He disclosed the details of his dream and the angel's words to him. Her eyes filled with tears, comforted to know that whatever reproach she would bear, that Joseph would bear it with her.

He listened with amazement when she told him that the angel Gabriel had called her *favored among all women.* The angel said that her baby boy was the Son of the Most High God, and that he would sit on the throne of his ancestor David and reign over Israel.

Joseph took her hands in his, asking God for the wisdom they both would need to begin making the right decisions for a future that clearly had no precedent.

Joseph wasted no time seeking out her father. The arrangements for their marriage were quickly made.

God would watch over His Word...

CHAPTER THREE

Mary grew more uncomfortable with each passing minute.

Every jolting step of the donkey sent yet another spasm of pain through her. She was sure the baby was coming and prayed they would make it to Bethlehem in time. The prophecies said the Messiah would be born in Bethlehem; she clung to that thought. She put her hand over her mouth, stifling a moan so that Joseph wouldn't hear her.

Joseph pressed forward, aware of her distress. She was slumped over and holding her belly; his mind rehearsed the possible scenarios of what could happen. He was also reminding himself where the messiah was prophesied to be born.

He jerked hard on the donkey's reins, instantly regretting that in his frustration he had added to Mary's discomfort. Bethlehem was just over the next hill, but a mile or so away. He had counted on having enough time to locate a relative or midwife; someone who could assist Mary when they got there.

The acrid smell of smoke drifted toward them. He realized with dismay that campsites were spread out around the parameter of the little town; it had never occurred to him that they might have to stay in the open, nor were they prepared. Bethlehem was so small it made sense now that there might not be room for all of the incoming people to have adequate shelter. Groups of people were huddled together around campfires, no more prepared than they were.

Mary slipped off the donkey. Joseph heard her gasp. Her eyes displayed her shock; she was standing in a steaming puddle of water. Adding to her discomfort, she was shivering uncontrollably. The baby would not wait. She began to cry.

Joseph slipped out of his robe and wrapped her in it. "God will provide for us, Mary," he told her. She nodded. God knew exactly where they were.

They walked slowly for Mary's sake. When they arrived at the outskirts of Bethlehem, Joseph ran ahead to see if he could find help for them. Mary took the donkey's reins from him, her acknowledgement that Joseph was exercising their last option.

It was evident that most of the villagers' homes had been seized by the Romans, having been converted into inns. This was but one of twelve villages that had been usurped by the Romans for the arbitrary census imposed on the Jews by Caesar Augustus to fund yet another extravagant building project.

In vain Joseph tried to find somewhere, anywhere to shelter his wife while she gave birth. His heart slammed into his chest with his increasing panic. He reminded himself again of who Mary was carrying. *He shall give His angels charge over us, to keep us in all our ways.* Once again he brought his thoughts under control.

He pounded on one door and then another. His efforts were greeted by muffed rebukes of 'Go away!" anonymously shouted at him from behind the closed doors. It was becoming stunningly clear that no one was willing to even inquire of him what might be the matter.

It was now dark and growing colder still. Joseph felt disoriented. He had been to Bethlehem before, but nothing looked the same. He had relatives who lived there, but everyone appeared to have been displaced by the takeover. If he and Mary had thought they had a plan, clearly it was now completely out of their own hands to accomplish it. Jehovah Jirah would provide.

Mary looked around frantically, trying to see where Joseph had gone. She sank to her knees, no longer able to stand, her contractions now coming at regular intervals, closer and closer all the time. She had never felt this frightened. Her teeth dug into her lower lip to hold back a scream; she tasted blood. *Where was Joseph?*

An old woman opened the door to Joseph's frantic pounding. She shook her head no, clearly annoyed at his intrusion, but curious enough to step outside to see what his problem was, having noted his panic. She looked around and saw a young woman slumped over on the ground; she then turned to watch Joseph running toward the next house. She looked from one and then back to the other, realizing with horror what was about to happen. She turned and disappeared inside to return seconds later shoving a reluctant husband towards Joseph while she went to Mary.

"Wait! Wait!" the man called after Joseph. Joseph paused, turning toward the most welcoming words he would ever hear. "There is a cave; I use it for a stable. It is only a short walk. It is all I have to offer you, but it will give you shelter tonight. Perhaps tomorrow you will find something better."

Joseph could have hugged him. He nodded his acceptance, momentarily unable to speak, returning to Mary who was on her feet and leaning heavily against her hostess. The old man grabbed the donkey's halter, leading them through Bethlehem and toward shelter.

Within minutes they stood at the entrance of a cave; one of many in the hills that surround Bethlehem.

The woman ducked inside with Mary and settled her in a pile of clean hay while simultaneously hollering orders to the men about what she needed them to bring her for Mary. "Go! Go quickly!" she yelled after them.

It wasn't long before the air was filled with the lusty cries of a healthy baby boy who protested his sudden change in environment. The old woman stepped into sight, holding aloft a steamy, wiggling infant.

She smiled a toothless smile at the waiting men, evidencing her own satisfaction at the happy ending before she returned to Mary with the newborn.

Joseph kindled a fire; her instructions for the next phase of what had to be done. It was a windless night; another blessing or the cave might fill with smoke. The woman reappeared, now making several trips with bundles of soiled hay and Mary's clothing that was beyond salvage, throwing it all on the greedy fire.

Joseph turned away to hide his tears of relief.

The Messiah had been born.

Mary lay on the straw, exhausted but exhilarated. She held the infant against her, the baby already having curled around her breast. Her eyes wandered over the tiny miracle in her arms. All mothers must share the wonder she was feeling, but she was required to factor into it the knowledge that God was reaching out to His people, and would do so through the babe she held against her. She thanked Him for the generous couple who had been willing to become involved in their situation; ministering angels in disguise.

The woman made clucking sounds to her animals; calming them after the intrusion at what should have been their mealtime. She threw armfuls of hay in front of them, and soon Mary was listening to the rhythmic sound of their chewing. The cave gave off the dungy, but comforting smells of occupation and Mary couldn't help but think that somehow it seemed fitting.

The woman took the baby out of Mary's reluctant grasp. It was time to swaddle him. She called for Joseph, who cautiously entered the cave carrying what Mary's mother had insisted they bring with them, having predicted that the baby would come before they returned home.

He spread out the linen wrappings on a blanket. The woman put the baby down in front of Joseph and held him still, instructing them on how he should be wrapped, starting with his shoulders. She told them to wrap him in sections, with the middle section wrapped separately so it could be unwound when the baby soiled himself. It was not a quick process, but finally he tucked the last strip of linen into the binding by the baby's feet.

Mary was thinking to herself that had anyone described this moment to her before tonight she would have told them they were crazy. Joseph rolled their baby back and forth, ignoring his pathetic whimpering, carefully following instructions. When they had finished, the baby looked like a little mummy; even his little head wrapped in linen.

Mary's heart was full. Until tonight she had thanked God for His provision in having given her this kind and gentle man for her husband. The extent to which Joseph had shown her kindness and mercy was beyond anything she could have imagined possible. Tonight, she knew that she loved him. His gentleness and faith in a good outcome had guided her through the frenzy and uncertainty just hours before. She had already forgotten the discomforts that had preceded the baby's birth

Joseph moved the manger away from the animals, turning it upside down to knock loose the remnants of feed that were stuck to it. He put it near where Mary was lying, filling it with clean hay. He took the stiff little parcel from the old woman and laid him in the manger, overwhelmed by the fierce protectiveness he felt for the only hours–old infant. The baby looked around, his eyes wide open; the only part of him he was able to move.

He turned to Mary who was watching him; neither of them able to find words to express what they were both feeling. The woman took this as her cue to leave, promising to check back in on them in the morning.

Joseph followed after her, trying to press some coins into her hand only to have them handed back to him. He blessed them both for their kindness and watched them disappear into the night, aware that God's timing had been perfect.

Suddenly Joseph was overwhelmed by his own exhaustion. Once he had satisfied himself that everything was in order, he dropped into a pile of hay near Mary. Within moments they were both asleep.

Somewhere in the distance they thought they could hear singing.

A bright light filled the cave, waking Joseph. He stood up, unable to ignore the unusual brightness. He put on his robe and stepped outside, wondering what its source was.

A group of what appeared to be shepherds made their way toward him. They were preceded by the pungent aroma that was a byproduct of their occupation. An elderly shepherd led them, wheezing and leaning heavily on his staff. Joseph couldn't imagine what might have prompted them to leave their flocks unattended in the middle of the night.

They were all talking at once, each one trying to be the first to tell Joseph why they had come. The odd ensemble of social outcasts gathered around him, excitedly talking over each other, telling him an unimaginable story about a host of angels who had appeared to them while they were tending their flocks; who sang to them of an infant king who had been born this very night; a king who would bring Shalom to the world.

"Is this where we will find Him?" they asked.

They pointed to the sky above Joseph; to the star that had positioned itself directly over the cave where his wife and child slept. This was the star they had followed to find the baby they were calling the savior of the world.

Mary peeked outside, wondering who Joseph could be talking to, fighting off a strangely disoriented feeling. She felt like she was playing a role in a drama; it all seemed so surreal. Joseph signaled that everything was all right, so she joined them. The shepherds were eager to tell Mary their story of why they had come.

Joseph went inside the cave and returned with the manger, setting it back down directly in front of the shepherds. Spontaneously they fell to their knees, overcome with emotion. They too had the feeling they were walking through a dream.

Joseph and Mary stood behind the manger, watching the shepherds straining to get a glimpse of the baby, comically shushing each other so as not to wake him. They could hear them sniffling; some were even audibly weeping; they were both stunned to witness such unabashed worship being offered to their son by men who were unclean by the standards of the law and would normally be shooed away. Jehovah had sent them to be the eye witnesses of the birth of His son, Immanuel.

The older shepherd compulsively reached out to touch the sleeping infant, instantly withdrawing his calloused and grime–caked hand, glancing at Mary with embarrassment. Mary leaned forward, letting him know that he was welcome to touch him. He bowed to her and immediately reached out again, allowing his forefinger to caress the downy cheek of the sleeping baby who woke at his touch, his mouth suddenly moving and making smacking sounds.

They all looked at each other, unable to suppress embarrassed smiles at the unmistakable reaction the newborn had to the touch on his cheek. One by one, the other shepherds took their turns touching the cheek of the tiny king.

Reluctantly they took their leave, each one passing by the manger one last time. Mary and Joseph recognized these men had left behind their livelihood to follow the star to where they were. They were the messengers who brought with them Heavenly confirmation of the holy event that had taken place in such obscurity. The many ironies of God's plan were not lost on Joseph.

Somewhere nearby a cock was crowing. The hazy pastel colors of dawn spread across the sky, obscuring the star. Joseph wondered if they would see it again.

Joseph carried the manger back into the cave, handing the now vigorously fussing baby to Mary. She opened her robe and drew the stiff little bundle inside her clothing and into her warmth.

Joseph sat next to her on the straw, incredulous that the baby was born and nestled between them. While the baby nursed, Joseph recounted for her the details of the amazing story told to him by the shepherds of the angel's instructions to follow the star, and who they said the shepherds would find.

The extraordinary events were another indication of the life chosen for them; one that would have little predictability, and possibly no permanence. Unorthodox as the events were as they continued to unfold, they knew that every detail was part of Jehovah's plan.

Joseph got up and rummaged through the provisions they had brought with them. He returned with a wineskin and some bread. He took the baby from Mary and lifted him aloft, committing him to God. He then blessed their food; their first meal as a family.

Soon they all slept; at rest under the shadow of The Almighty.

CHAPTER FOUR

Joseph stood over Mary and the sleeping child in the dark room hating that he must wake her. Watching her sleeping he realized that even at rest Mary's body was curled around their son, cocooning him protectively.

The events of the last several days had taken their toll on her. The amazing circumstances had weighed heavily on him as well, but Joseph's ability to appear calm was Mary's assurance of their son's safety and that was paramount for her to be able to retain a sense of normalcy in their complicated life together.

Silently he prayed, *I stand over them, Lord, placing us in the secret place of your presence and protection. Most High God, I trust you and I know we are safe under your wings. No matter where you send us, no matter what you ask of us, we will do it for your sake and the sake of your people. I rest in your safekeeping knowing your mercies are new every morning.*

He leaned over, gently shaking her awake. Mary's eyes opened, but she didn't move. While her eyes adjusted to the darkness, she realized that Joseph was already dressed. They must be going somewhere, and quickly! He was already fully clothed, with his outer garment over his tunic, belted with his leather pouch secured at his waist. Before she could say anything, he put his finger to his lips so she didn't disturb Jesus.

She disengaged herself from Jesus's sleeping body, allowing Joseph to help her to her feet. Her clothes were laid out and folded on the bed. Joseph picked them up and handed them to her, leaving her to get dressed while he tethered their donkey and her colt that were penned behind the house. No words were exchanged; none were necessary.

Mary fumbled with her clothes, instinctively realizing haste was involved. She looked around and saw that Joseph had already put out additional bundles of clothing, blankets; skins of water, along with their treasures from the Magi by the door. She didn't want to think about what it all might mean.

Her thoughts were interrupted by the sounds of Joseph leading the donkeys around to the front of the house. She could hear him whispering to them; keeping them calm so they wouldn't wake the neighbors.

What they didn't need was more attention. The last few days were like walking through a dream, and not necessarily a good one. She realized the seriousness of the moment in Joseph's care to escape with his family in the stealth of night.

Mary had developed the ability to categorize her memories, pretending for the moment that it might be possible for them to have a normal life. After months of trying to establish a routine in their marriage, she was once again dealing with the awareness she must constantly be on guard for the unexpected events that might happen at any minute of every day.

Joseph and Mary had been required by law to appear at the Temple after the birth of their baby. According to God's covenant with Abraham a son was to be circumcised on the eighth day after his birth; he would be given his name at that time, also. They had purchased two doves for Mary's purification after childbirth as well; people of means would have offered a lamb or a kid.

After the troublesome encounters with Simeon and Anna at the Temple, Joseph searched out Elizabeth's husband, Zechariah, who lived in a small town on the outskirts of Jerusalem. Joseph trusted that he and Elizabeth would be able to help them with the decisions they urgently needed to make about what they should do next, being deliberately cautious about rushing into anything.

Zechariah's own supernatural visitation by the angel Gabriel in the Temple telling him of the unexpected blessing of a baby who would be born to them years after they should have been able to conceive boosted both Mary and Joseph's faith; confirming to them God's larger plan for their son.

They accepted Zechariah's invitation to stay in the safety of their home. Because of their protection, Mary and Joseph relished the opportunity to share their story with the only two people who could begin to understand the perplexing dynamics surrounding the births of the baby cousins and how each of their sons fit into the prophecies regarding God's promises to His people.

Their newborn seemed fragile when laid beside his older cousin. John was a strapping baby boy with dark, wiry hair that stuck out in every direction. He was active and extremely vocal, already exhibiting a precocious personality. By comparison, Jesus was a model baby.

Once asked, Zechariah did not withhold his strong opinions, urging Joseph to not return to Nazareth with Mary and the baby. He told him that he had been concerned for many years about the overlapping dynamics of the Temple politics and Rome's persecution of the Jews. After the birth of his own baby, he was even more alert to the rumors and manipulations that constantly went on around him.

Because of his wise council Joseph convinced Mary they should return to Bethlehem instead of going home. Mary and Joseph's families had been relieved with their decision to marry immediately, but there would have been merciless speculation from Nazareth's other residents once they began to ask questions. Joseph did not wish to stir the pot of controversy. To maintain their anonymity was vital.

Elizabeth assured Mary that she would personally get word to her mother that she had seen the baby and that Mary was safe even if she had to travel there herself. She was adamant that it was best only a few knew about the details of the baby's origin or where the couple lived lest the child's destiny be discovered outside of God's timing. Zechariah further cautioned Joseph to not return to the Temple. He was adamant that even the well–intended might prove dangerous to the couple and their infant son.

Before they left for Bethlehem, Elizabeth and Zechariah generously supplied them with gifts and some basic necessities to help them begin their life in their first home. Mary was thrilled with the blankets, shawls, utensils, oil, and spices that Elizabeth bundled together the day they left. Elizabeth offered Mary some of her own clothing, noticing the young woman had only one garment to wear. Mary was moved to tears, knowing that her mother would be comforted when she heard of her cousin's kindness to her.

Zechariah gave Joseph some clothes, along with some scrolls, and a bottle of fine oil used for anointing. He presented him with a seamless robe of fine linen, a gift from him for Joseph's son one day.

Just before they left Elizabeth took Mary with her to her garden where they dug up roots and bulbs, wrapping them in damp cloths to insure they would survive the journey and could be planted later. Mary was elated to be able to have her own garden once they were settled into a house.

Joseph and Mary left them early on a crisp, cloudless morning heading south to Bethlehem.

They began making plans for their life together, giving themselves permission to be excited for the first time.

J oseph found a small house where he could settle his family.

Once it was discovered that he was a carpenter he instantly had work; more work than he could handle. He could have worked day and night had he chosen to. Mary happily occupied herself by making the little house their home.

The enrollment of Joseph's clan had turned the little town of Bethlehem into a virtual circus. The residents had been compelled to stand aside while the Roman soldiers confiscated whatever they needed to provide for the needs of the continuing stream of people arriving (along with their animals), all requiring to be housed and fed.

Most of the citizens of Bethlehem's homes had been seized and turned into temporary inns used for the accommodations of the soldiers and tax collectors. The Jews who had been compelled to journey from long distances had found themselves on their own to find shelter wherever they could, many having been forced to sleep in the open.

When the dust from the occupation had settled and everyone had left, the small town was turned inside out. Few residents had either the time or the energy to think twice about the rumors of shepherds or their story of angels who sent them to find a baby who would bring peace to the world. Their total preoccupation was to regain some normalcy while they put their disrespected lives back in order.

Mary and Joseph were temporarily anonymous and happy to be so.

Except...

Except for the star, the bright terrestrial oddity that had appeared in the sky over Bethlehem during the census and had not disappeared since. Eventually the villagers adjusted to its presence over their town but since it did not seem to hasten any ominous events it had become less a topic of interest.

But Mary and Joseph could not forget how the star had been the beacon by which the shepherds had found their son. The star's presence remained as a nightly reminder to them of how fragile their current obscurity was. It was impossible for Mary not to be reminded of the strange events that had placed them in Bethlehem for their son's birth, remembering the words of the prophet Micah about the one that God said He would send who would be born there.

Their little boy grew, delighting them with his happy disposition and loving nature. Mary's heart ached to not be able to share him with

Joseph's or her families, but she had accepted that it would be unwise for them to travel to Nazareth. So, she busied herself instead with the task of setting up their household.

Although she longed for friends and family who would have eagerly shared with her from their own experiences how to care for her son, loneliness was an indulgence she chose not to embrace. Nothing was going to rob her of this precious time with her little boy. She indulged herself the extravagance of hours when she did nothing but watch him while he slept, trying to commit to memory every detail of how he looked; overcome with how much she loved him.

Joseph had more than enough work to keep him busy, but because he adored his wife and little boy, he stole every possible moment to be with them.

Theirs was not a honeymoon, but they became a couple; both of them treasuring this time of bonding with their child and with each other.

Although they took little notice of it, the star had slowly begun moving until it came to rest directly above their little house, its beam a beacon to an entourage of mystics who had travelled from the east and had been following it with great interest. These were the wise men, students of astronomy and ancient prophecies, who were intrigued by the sudden appearance of this unusual star and its possible meanings. For months they had been traveling in search of the child who the prophecies foretold would become a Jewish King who would bring peace to the world.

Their travels eventually brought them uninvited to the simple doorway of the carpenter and his family.

Their passage through the town of Bethlehem was a most curious parade of ornately adorned camels, the Mystics from the Orient dressed in their royal regalia, and a large company of servants. Their arrival created both consternation and curiosity; consternation was inevitable because the village had finally returned to some sense of normalcy and its citizens wanted nothing to do with anything that might disrupt their newly regained sense of peace; to not be curious would have been impossible.

So, late one night Mary and Joseph were abruptly awakened by the loud commotion created by this odd entourage whose destination ended in their front yard. Joseph hastened outside to meet them, and after learning about their determination to find them he invited them into their home where Mary waited with their drowsy son.

The Magi fell to their knees to worship the child. They presented him with caskets that contained gifts that were extravagant by anyone's standards. Mary had no previous experience to help her process either the value or significance of their offerings to her son.

They quickly recognized the vulnerability of the child. Having been detained by Herod on their way through Jerusalem they regretted they had told him their destination or who it was they were seeking. Before leaving Bethlehem they warned Joseph that Herod had been far too interested in their whereabouts.

Realizing that his family had been exposed Joseph's mind raced while he instinctively began to put a plan together for them to flee, trusting God for a sign before he did anything that might further jeopardize his family.

He would not have to wait long.

J oseph and Mary stood side by side in the moonlight, looking around the little plot of land that had been so briefly theirs. Joseph deposited the sleepy little boy on the donkey's back, tucking him securely under a blanket between the bundles he had tied there, deliberately creating a little bed.

They offered God their future, leaving behind their life in Bethlehem.

Joseph reached out and took Mary's hand in his, squeezing it gently. He told her that God had instructed him in another dream to leave Bethlehem immediately and escape with his family to Egypt.

The moment Joseph had committed himself to taking care of Mary and to the unborn child, Mary had placed herself in his care with no conditions. It didn't matter where they went, because her only safety was her complete trust in God's provision for her and their son in Joseph. She squeezed his hand in return; transferring to him her unspoken gratitude and faith in his decision to flee.

As they made their way into the unknown, prodded along by another dream, from the north a legion of Roman soldiers galloped toward the sleeping village of Bethlehem. The paranoia of King Herod and his fear that a little boy might usurp his kingdom would again crush the sleeping town. By the dawn's light, the blood of the innocents would soak the dusty streets.

The only fanfare to their departure was the sound of crickets chirping in the night.

Joseph looked behind him one last time.

The star had disappeared.

CHAPTER FIVE

Joseph deliberately slowed his pace while walking toward home one hot, cloudless afternoon. He was relishing the moment. From the pocket of his tunic, he withdrew a squirming little puppy. He brought her up to his nose, breathing in her sweet smell.

It was the natal day of their son Jesus and he had been anticipating this moment ever since he had noticed a litter of pups behind a shed he was repairing. He asked them if he could have one for his son and they had kept her for Joseph to claim on this special day. Joseph inhaled her delicious scent one more time, picturing his son's reaction when he saw her.

Mary's days were now occupied in caring for another baby son. Baby James was more demanding than Jesus had been, and Mary no longer had the luxury of time to spend playing with his big brother. Isolated by both language and culture, their exile was felt far more extremely because of Mary's continual caution to allow Jesus out of her sight, if even for a moment.

Rumors of the slaughter of the male children in Bethlehem had inevitably reached them. Mentally Mary was always prepared to flee again for their son's safety. Although Jesus had quickly learned the new language, it was out of the question for him to be allowed to play out of her sight. She hoped the puppy would be a good diversion for him and would also give him some responsibility.

Joseph neared their street. He stopped short of the corner, peeking toward their small brick house. Jesus was standing and facing his mother who was seated on a stool in front of their home, shaded by a wide canvas awning. Jesus was hopping up and down, puffs of dust rising from his feet when he landed. Mary laughed; obviously enjoying the entertainment Jesus was providing due to his uncontainable excitement.

The sound of Mary's laughter was like music in his ears. The months of adjusting to the total isolation imposed on her in this strange land, compounded by her sadness at not being able to get word to anyone about what had happened to them had changed her. He felt the isolation as well, and it weighed heavily on him. But, when he arrived home from a day's work, he put aside his own weariness to play with his children and enjoy them with his wife, knowing she had waited all day for this time together as a family.

Jesus's excitement shouldn't be wasted; Joseph didn't want to lose the desired effect should the baby began fussing. He shook his head at the thought of the imponderable events that had taken place this same day several years earlier; events that became more overwhelming with time.

Stepping back out of sight, he lowered the wiggling little bundle of fur back into his pocket, resting his hand against her to quiet her while she wiggled up against it. "Shhhhh, little puppy! It won't be long!" he whispered.

He stepped out and rounded the corner toward home, picking up his pace as he walked toward his family. He couldn't help but revel in a job well done.

When Mary saw him approaching she leaned over and lifted James from his basket and sat him on her lap. Even the baby should get to see Jesus receive his exciting gift!

Jesus resumed his animated hopping; now hopping from one foot to the other, clapping his hands together in anticipation of his papa's return.

Mary pointed at Joseph; immediately Jesus galloped toward him. .

Abruptly he stopped, aware that Joseph wasn't carrying anything. He looked quizzically at Joseph, then back toward his mama, then back at Joseph's empty hands, causing Joseph to momentarily wonder if he had overdone the secrecy. Jesus decided he would just wait to see what would happen next. His papa had promised him a surprise. His papa would never break a promise.

Joseph told him to "Sit down by your mama, and close your eyes as tightly as you can." Jesus sped back to Mary, sitting down at her knees, closing his eyes ever so tightly. Joseph smiled when he saw Jesus's wiggling feet that were protesting more waiting.

"Now hold out your hands," Joseph said. Jesus hands popped out, palms up.

Joseph lowered the wiggling puppy into Jesus waiting hands, his little fingers immediately wrapping themselves around her. Jesus's eyes were still closed; he opened them one at a time, slowly taking in this amazing gift. The puppy's exuberant tail was evidence at her own delight with her new master, his happy giggles erupting when his new playmate began kissing his hands and face as he fell backwards on the ground.

Hugging their baby to her, Mary watched the magic of Joseph's long–awaited presentation unfolding before her. She thanked God for the provision of this wonderful man who gave so selflessly to them and asked nothing for himself. She looked from Jesus and the puppy to her husband in time to see a tear roll down Joseph's cheek and disappear into his beard.

Joseph's eyes met hers. It was a perfect day!

CHAPTER SIX

I t was time that Jesus knew his kinsmen. Mary never spoke of her loneliness, but it added to Joseph's sense of urgency to return to Nazareth. He waited on God, asking Him for the signal that it was His time for him to return to their homeland. As the angel had promised, Joseph was again visited by an angel in a dream who assured him that Herod was dead and it was now safe to begin planning for their journey home.

Joseph wondered if their mysterious disappearance after the census might still be an ongoing controversy. It was hard to imagine it that it would have been forgotten. He wasn't sure what he and Mary could say to explain the years of absence, but he knew that God would give them wisdom to know what they should reveal.

It was a luxury to be able to anticipate what they would need for the return trip home. Joseph was able to sell or trade most of their possessions, obtaining another donkey for them. This time he knew what he was preparing them for. The weight of the boy's future rested on his shoulders and he could not forget for a moment who it was that he had been asked to adopt. He threw himself fully on God's faithfulness, knowing they would not be tested without a way of escape. Even then, he didn't discount the possibility that before they reached Nazareth they might well have tasted manna. It was his job to be prepared and trust God to do the rest.

Since they would be returning to Nazareth, he hoped they would not be starting over from nothing. Joseph had left behind a house, and he felt it would be there in some shape or form. He counted on his brother–in–law, Judas, to have looked after it with the hope of their return. His sister would have fiercely clung to that hope.

The simple thought of returning to a place where they had friends and family was an emotional luxury; to celebrate Sabbath's with family would be like heaven itself. His sister was good hearted and selfless, and Joseph was counting on her help in Mary's transition to resuming their life there. He knew that she would help them get settled and buffer Mary from any unpleasant intrusions.

Sadly, he knew that her adjustment would not be without complications. Mary's parents had been frail when he and Mary left for the census in Bethlehem, and it was likely their worries about what had happened to Mary and the baby would have been overwhelming for them; that along with the effect the rumors about Mary's pregnancy would have had on their own reputations. They would have been sure to hear what had happened to the babies in Bethlehem. He grieved to think of their families having to deal with the obvious speculations of what might have happened to them at the hand of Herod.

Jesus helped Joseph stack their belongings in front of their house. Joseph showed him how he was going to tie them on the donkeys so there would be a level place for him and his mother to ride. The third donkey would carry their provisions.

Jesus asked his papa where he would ride; Joseph said that he would walk.

Joseph rigged it so poles could be erected so that he could stretch skins over Jesus and Mary to protect them from the sun's merciless scorching. Joseph dreaded the long walk, thinking of the Exodus. The Israelites' clothes and shoes had not worn out during their forty years of wandering. He assumed their feet hadn't either.

Joseph practiced shooting his sling shot and put it where he could easily access it. He did not wish to worry Mary, but there were bandits, and even animals who preyed on travelers who had been weakened by the sun and lack of water.

Joseph reminded himself of God's provision for His people in the wilderness. *Jehovah Jirah, God will provide,* he murmured. Yes, God would provide. Joseph's cargo was entangled with eternal destiny. He struggled to understand it, and he could not. But, whenever his hand rested upon the curly head of the little boy who called him "Abba", he humbly thanked God for the providence that had chosen him to instruct the lad in the ways of God.

Before they began their journey, Joseph gathered his little family inside their home; its stark emptiness testified to the finality of the moment. He prayed, thanking God for bringing them here, away from danger and for His many blessings while they were there. He took some oil, tenderly anointing each member of his family; he anointed himself last.

Mary was unable to refrain from weeping when the full reality of leaving hit her. She was leaving behind the mementoes of another baby's birth, all of their furniture, toys, and utensils that Joseph had made for her that now must be relegated to memories; memories carefully stored so that she could one day tell her sons stories about their time of exile in Egypt and that they had been happy there.

Mary had grown to love her neighbors despite the frustrating obstacles of language, custom, and her own caution. She knew they would never see each other again, and had put aside mementos for each one from her most treasured possessions to present to them upon their leaving so they would have something by which to remember the carpenter's family.

With the help of his papa, Jesus had whittled little statues of lambs to give each of his little friends. Jesus's only memories up until now were the time they had spent living there. He realized that his life was about to change forever.

Joseph's plan was for them to leave in the early evening when the sun's brutal heat would not hinder them from getting a good start. Time was slipping away, and Joseph was becoming impatient to be underway.

Mary stood hand in hand with her neighbors. They studied at each other intently, committing to memory the details of each face and dress. Their tears fell without embarrassment, the silent offering of unspoken love and respect. These precious women had added a dimension to her life that had been unexpected and unforgettable; the sweet aroma of their gained trust and love would linger for a lifetime.

Joseph took her by the arm, gently pulling her away with her neighbors rushing after her with gifts of food and small remembrances for Jesus and James. Kind hands released them to the journey ahead with Jesus walking backwards, waving both hands at them; waving until his friends were but tiny specks in the now dusky landscape. He was sad, but home for Him was His complete trust in the two people who were leading Him away.

He turned around to feel his papa's strong hands lifting him. In the cradle of Joseph's arms, he was carried into the unknown, resting contentedly against the rhythmic beating of his father's heart.

They encountered driving winds the second day.

There was no protection from the relentless, gritty sand that pummeled them. Joseph was finally forced to give in to it. He halted his little caravan, wrapping the donkey's heads to protect their eyes and noses from the sand, making them lie down so they could use them to buffer them against the sandstorm.

Lastly, he pulled skins over them, using his own body to help shield them. Even then they could barely breathe, constantly aware of the sand that was accumulating in drifts around them.

Joseph feared they were far off course.

Their skin was raw and was chafed from the sand's relentless abrasion. A small blessing was that the clouds of swirling sand kept the sun from scorching them by day. To talk had become torture, their lips chapped and cracked. Even baby James finally ceased to cry, his throat and lungs on fire from taking in the hostile air.

On the fourth day the wind stopped as suddenly as it had begun. They jumped up to throw off the uncomfortable coverings and stretch their stiff limbs looking above them at a blue and cloudless sky.

Mary and Joseph vigorously shook the dust out of their blankets and clothing. They had not eaten once they realized that to merely uncover their food was to expose it to the gritty particles in the air, rendering it inedible. Finally, they could quiet their rumbling stomachs.

In the shadows of the donkeys, they rested on skins, picnicking on cheese and dates and sipping warm but refreshing water. The simple meal refreshed both their bodies and spirits; once again they could look to being on their way with a degree of excitement.

Joseph handed Jesus bundles of grass for him to throw in front of the donkeys. They watched, fascinated that the donkeys were able to carefully separate each blade with their nimble lips, somehow managing to not eat the sand with it.

There wasn't enough water for them to wash, so Mary sparingly dampened a cloth and folded it so they each could at least each use a corner of the rag that was not dirty to wipe away some of the grime. After they had each taken their turn, they realized they had exposed white circles around their eyes and mouths in contrast to the grime left on their faces. It was Jesus who laughed first. His mirth at their appearances was contagious, and soon they were all laughing uncontrollably at how silly they each looked.

It was time to press on. Joseph calculated they had lost two days. Mary sat on one donkey with the baby while Jesus straddled the other; the dog following close behind. Joseph silently shouldered the concern that their provisions might not last until they were safely across the wilderness. He replaced his worries with promises from the scriptures. Instantly he felt peace.

Joseph and Mary made the time pass more quickly for Jesus by telling him stories.

Jesus understood what the Passover was. While in Egypt they had kept the Passover, using their exile there to help Jesus understand who Moses was and how God used him to liberate the Jewish people from slavery.

Joseph reminded them again how on the night of Passover each family was told to kill a lamb and to put its blood on the top and sides of their doorways to protect them from the angel of death that would pass through Egypt that night. That night they were instructed to stay inside and eat the lamb. In the morning they would pass through the blood-marked doorways having been passed over for judgment and set aside as a people God had set apart for Himself.

Their Passover celebrations in Egypt had taken on a depth of meaning and would be richer now for their having traveled across the wilderness toward the land promised their forefathers. After the Jews fled Egypt they wandered for forty years in this same unforgiving landscape, holding on to the promise that God was bringing them to a land flowing with milk and honey.

Joseph described the many miracles God did for them; how God pushed back the waters of the Red Sea, how He had gone before them as a swirling cloud by day, and followed behind them as a tower of fire by night. Mary told him how God provided water from a rock for them when they were thirsty, and gave them bread that fell like dew from Heaven called "manna".

Their words drew a vivid picture of the vast company of people who continually tested Moses and God; most of them who died in the wilderness because of their rebellion; even Moses would not be able to enter into the Promised Land with them. But, the Jewish people became a nation during the forty years God set them apart in the wilderness.

Because Joshua and Caleb did not doubt God's ability to deliver the land to them they were the only two people from their generation who would enter the land promised to Abraham.

Jesus pretended to be Joshua, taking big steps and claiming the land for the Lord.

Jesus loved the stories and wore Joseph out with his requests of, "Tell me another one," and "One more time, please, Papa!"

It was a long and arduous journey, but rich because the little family identified with their God and His promises for His people, Israel.

They found Jehovah true.

CHAPTER SEVEN

With difficulty, Joseph exhibited a demeanor of calm that he did not feel. The brutal landscape had taken its toll on all of them, both physically and emotionally. Every muscle in Joseph's body screamed with fatigue. He hoped that Mary had not yet surmised their critically low supply of food and water…

The Lord is my shepherd, I shall not want; the Lord is my shepherd, I shall not want … he thought, longing for green pastures and still waters in the shelter of a valley.

Mary focused on the baby, having already suspected that they were running out of food. She withheld from Joseph that her milk had all but dried up; the baby now pacified purely by his contact with her. James' chubbiness was gone, and she was sure that his sleepiness was because of lack of food and not contentment, his little tummy distended and tender to the touch. He had ceased to cry. She realized that Joseph had enough challenges without her adding to them by voicing her concerns; there was nothing he could do. She recited the words from Isaiah to herself, *For the Lord shall comfort Zion: He will comfort all her waste places; and make her wilderness like the garden of the Lord; joy and gladness shall be found therein, thanksgiving, and the voice of melody.*

She replaced her fears with God's words for His people.

Even Jesus plodded along with his head down, his silence testimony to his own fatigue.

Mary knew that when his endless barrage of questions had ceased that he must be experiencing the same hypnotic weariness that the never–ending barrenness instilled.

Mary chose to walk to ease the burden of her emaciated donkey. They walked slowly with their heads down to shield their eyes from the burning sun. Each step had become a purposeful commitment toward being home. As the sun sank in the west, the little family blended into the landscape looking like slowly moving statues in a setting of sepia tones.

They trudged over a dune to see the silhouettes of palm trees off in the distance. Mary's knees became weak; she almost fainted with relief to know the worst would soon be behind them. They were still a half day's walk away, but Joseph knew the trees signaled that water was within reach. When they finally stopped to rest that night, they closed their eyes knowing that the dawn would bring with it the end of their futility. They would soon be entering the Promised Land.

Joseph woke before dawn. He sat with his knees drawn up under his chin, his head covered in his prayer shawl, looking toward the distant hills, now bathed in the golden glow of dawn, murmuring softly the words of David: "Lift thine eyes toward the hills from which cometh my help, my help cometh from the Lord…" Today he was able to appreciate the delicate infusion of color that preceded the sun's arrival; before today he had dreaded it, being able to think only of its sadistic scorching.

He had never doubted God's faithfulness for a moment; his gratitude to experience God's stunning provision for his family overwhelmed him. He couldn't imagine how Moses must have felt when he saw the Promised Land in the distance, knowing that after forty years of wandering in the wilderness he would not be the one who would lead his people in.

Joseph had never doubted God's faithfulness but he had begun to wonder what they would have to go through before it was over.

When he looked at his still sleeping family he sensed the overriding love God had for man and his yearning for fellowship with him. God was again reaching out to his people. *Please, God, prepare your people to accept what you are offering them.*

Once they were all awake, Joseph laid out the remainder of their meager supplies on a blanket, aware that God had known exactly what they would need.

He bowed his head and thanked God for His provision. They slowly chewed the last of the hard, dry cheese and shriveled figs, wondering if they had enough saliva to be able to swallow what they were eating; there was no more water.

They got up and wordlessly looked toward the shimmering hills, now aware there was movement in the distance. They looked closely and could make out the familiar shape of camels moving toward them. That sight was enough to inspire Jesus to call to his dog and run on ahead of them.

Joseph was barely able to force himself to move, but he grimly picked up their pace so that his family could rest in shade while he found a well to water their donkeys, now walking skeletons.

Mary wept soundlessly, holding the baby up in front of her so Joseph would not see her crying. She wept, her body unable to produce tears.

But, she was weeping for joy. Soon they would be home.

CHAPTER EIGHT

The terrain now required them to climb up and then down the steep, rocky slopes that led to Galilee. Goats and sheep dotted the hillsides, and an occasional eagle soared high above them. Absolutely everything held within it the magic of being seen by them as if for the first time. They had finally returned to the land that flowed with milk and honey.

They were somewhat refreshed, having replenished food and drink, but still dirty and bedraggled, having made the choice to keep moving rather than delay for another moment their goal to be home. Joseph and Mary pushed themselves so they could finally put the long trip behind them. A new addition to their family was a female goat, led by Jesus. Milk had been welcomed by the two hungry little boys, and she became a comical distraction while they watched Jesus trying to outmaneuver her when she lowered her head to butt him; stubbornly resisting being pulled along by a rope.

Clusters of date palms appeared, fields of budding grape vines, along with the gnarled shapes of olive trees that grew in groves on the hillsides. Along the road were fig trees, ladened with green fruit, and interspersed with almond trees that hummed with the sound of bees collecting nectar from their sweet pink blossoms. The vivid hues of wildflowers painted the hillsides, reminding them that they had not merely imagined a world where color existed. Birds sang out their joyous celebration of springtime.

Their memories stirred as their wilderness experience gave way to the rediscovery of what once had been familiar. The atmosphere was infused with the intoxicating scents of springtime. Mary and Joseph breathed in the fragrant air; certain that no perfume could ever compare to it. Everything they had left behind was suddenly a new discovery, and they noticed every detail.

Their excitement to being back in Galilee was suddenly turned to horror. Without warning the harsh reminders of the cruel occupation of the Romans accosted them. Naked bodies, tied or nailed to crosses and trees, suddenly became part of the landscape.

Those who had been executed were exhibited in differing stages of decomposition and contamination depending on their accessibility to prowling animals; there was no way to protect them from the birds. Most of the corpses left on display had no families, and if they did, they had ceased to be able to be recognizable.

Mary put her shawl over her head and face, and pulled it over the baby. She clutched him close to her, pressing her shawl over her own nose hoping to prevent any further invasion of her senses. She choked back an involuntary sob to think of the suffering displayed with the intent to intimidate.

Joseph attempted to shield Jesus from the atrocities after passing by the first of the crosses, intended by Rome to be unavoidable. *How could he have forgotten about the horrifying symbols of cruelty?*

Jesus's reaction to them was to recoil in shock, such violence being completely foreign to him. He was silent and Joseph was concerned what effect the gory visages might have on his sensitive son.

Jesus drew close to his father, silently processing what he had just seen. He obeyed without question when Joseph suggested it might be better if he kept his eyes focused straight ahead of him and not look to the right or left. But, the sights and smells demanded explanations that could not be ignored.

He finally demanded that Joseph explain to him what could cause such cruelty to be transferred from one human to another. *What could these people have done to deserve such a cruel death?*

Eventually Joseph found a place of reprieve away from the roadway in a grove of trees and attempted to explain to him how God's people had suffered persecution many times, and reminded him of God's promise to one day send a redeemer who would return the world to how God intended it to be when God created man.

He watched Jesus's reactions while he meticulously and deliberately chose each word. *God of Abraham, Isaac, and Jacob, grant me wisdom to know what to say,* he whispered to himself.

Jesus's eyes held his father's, barely blinking. His head nodded when his father told him of the promise of the one God promised to send to rescue His people. Joseph looked into their depths and wondered to himself how their little boy could possibly process his feeble explanations at such inhumanity.

After sitting in silence for some time, Jesus spoke, "He will come, Papa."

"Who will come?" asked Joseph.

The boy solemnly answered, "The One."

Joseph simply said, "Yes, Jesus. He will."

He avoided looking into his son's eyes, turning away from him to get ready to continue their journey.

Silently they resumed their journey toward Nazareth.

CHAPTER NINE

I t was Joseph's nephews who spotted them first. When Joseph saw the young men approaching, he recognized them immediately. His gaze was met with their stares, followed by a collective gasp when the boys one by one realized who it was that was coming toward them. They turned and sped back toward Nazareth to tell their mother that Joseph had come home.

Within moments, a small entourage of excited relatives ran toward them. Ruth was in the lead, her tunic pulled in front of her between her legs so she could run. No one else was going to be the first to embrace her brother!

"Joseph! Mary! A little boy! A baby?" Ruth could not believe her eyes. Her brother was alive! He and Mary had returned home! She threw herself into Joseph's arms, laughing and crying at the same time, almost knocking him over in her excitement. God had heard her prayers. Joseph was back!

Each of them was individually embraced, examined, and exclaimed over. Judas took the donkeys leads from Joseph and began leading the sad looking beasts toward the village to unpack and feed them. Jesus went with him, leading their resistant goat. His dog begrudgingly followed; unwilling to leave her master but longing to lie down somewhere and lick her sore paws.

Joseph followed behind, wincing at the relentless pain in his feet. Judas slowed his pace, putting his arm around his brother-in-law's shoulders, prompted to assure him that the taxes on his house had been paid in faith that they one day would return. Joseph sagged with relief to know the efforts of his heart and hands toward Mary still remained because of Judas' faith that God would bring them back safely.

Ruth took the baby out of Mary's arms and handed him over to one of her daughters, suggesting she find Jesus and take the children to the stream to let them play and splash off some of the dirt from their travels.

Now it was Mary's turn. Ruth took her by the hand and led her home.

Mary gave herself completely over to the gracious hospitality of her sister–in–law. The conspicuous absence of word about her family made Mary sad, but for the moment she would hold at bay any shadows that might cloud the blessing of being so joyously welcomed home. She knew Ruth would wait for the right moment to introduce that reality into her homecoming.

Once home, Ruth found a clean shift of her own to exchange for the tattered one Mary was wearing. She laid it out along with a towel, a comb, some oil, and a bowl of fresh water. Ruth left the house, sensing that Mary could use some time by herself to process her thoughts. There would be plenty of time to catch up, although she was jumping up and down on the inside trying to contain the questions that had haunted her for so long.

Mary was grateful for a few moments of solitude. She bowed her head over the bowl of water thinking of how luxurious something so simple seemed to her at this moment. She thanked God again for His faithfulness; not just for the water, but that through this time of trusting Him she now saw His goodness in even the smallest details. She would take nothing for granted ever again; of that she was certain. Whatever they had suffered was a small price to have paid for the unspeakable joy of their homecoming.

She rinsed off her face and neck, watching the water turn dark from the grime that was embedded in her skin. Mary cringed when she noticed the comb and reached up to touch her hopelessly matted hair, sure that it would need to be cut away and grow back before she needed a comb again.

Mary poured some of the olive oil onto her hands, feeling it immediately soften her dry, cracked skin; the instant result soothing her spirit as well. She patted some on her face, trying not to think about how she must look to anyone else. The next day she would go to the stream, now full from the spring rains, and soak away the dirt from their travels. But, tonight she would sleep with her husband under a roof in clean clothes. Her babies would be clean and safe when she tucked them into bed. Joseph could at last rest. And they would not be hungry.

They were home.

It seemed like a dream.

Ruth entered the house with a basket hoisted on her hip, filled with vegetables from her garden. Immediately she began preparing a meal for her weary guests.

She declined Mary's offer to help. Instead she pulled up a stool, informing Mary that her job was to relax and answer her questions about what had happened since she and Joseph had left for Bethlehem.

Mary was overwhelmed to actually be having a conversation with another woman. She began by describing their journey to Bethlehem and Joseph's frantic search for a place where she could have their baby. Ruth was incredulous when Mary told her how shepherds had found them after following a star to where they were and what the angels had told them. Tears stung her eyes when she tried to put into words the tender and protective care shown to her by Joseph and his selflessness over the course of time that had at long last brought them back to their family.

It wasn't long before Judas appeared at the door. He removed his sandals and hung his robe on a peg outside before entering. Joseph followed close behind, pausing outside to take off his robe. Although it was dirty and tattered, he shook it off and folded it carefully before laying it on the ground outside the doorway. He bent over and slowly removed his sandals.

Judas gasped! His brother–in–law's feet were raw. Joseph's sandals fell away, exposing open and bleeding sores. *How was it possible for Joseph to have completed the journey?* Obviously it was because of his determination to bring his family home again at whatever cost to himself.

Judas placed a stool on the floor in front of Joseph. Joseph gratefully succumbed to the invitation to finally be off his feet. He covered his feet as best as he could with the hem of his tunic, hoping no one had noticed them.

Judas turned toward Ruth who had also witnessed Joseph removing his sandals; she was already pouring water into a bowl. She offered it to Judas along with a clean towel that she draped over his arm. Instead of handing the bowl and towel to Joseph, Judas got down on his knees in front of him and placed the bowl between them on the floor.

When Jesus had noticed his father going toward the house he followed him. He neared the doorway just in time to see his uncle kneel down in front of his papa. He watched his uncle lift Joseph's tunic and drape it over his knees and one at a time take each of Joseph's feet into his hands and pour clean water over them, tenderly washing away the blood and dirt.

Joseph lowered his head to receive this offered dignity, overcome with love for the one who offered it to him.

Jesus watched his aunt place her hands on Mary's shoulders; both women moved to tears by Judas' humble gesture of compassion. Jesus edged forward toward his father, watching his uncle pour oil and wine over the wounds on Joseph's feet and wrap them in strips of linen.

Jesus reached out and put his hands on each of Joseph's shoulders as he had seen his aunt do with his mother. Joseph felt the small hands, reminded again of the role he was called to be to the boy.

Judas's simple act of kindness would be called to remembrance by Joseph's family whenever they recalled their own exodus from Egypt.

CHAPTER TEN

J esus followed his father to the edge of their village and watched him walk away, heading into the hills outside Nazareth. Every time Joseph left to go on one of his vigils, Jesus begged to go along. "Soon, son; soon you can come." Joseph told him. But, tonight Joseph went alone; he needed this time with the Lord.

The sun was setting. Jesus returned to the workshop alone. It was now his responsibility to put away their tools and to sweep up after a day's work. Jesus quickly finished his chores before his mother called him to supper.

It was intriguing to think about what made Joseph look forward to going away by himself all night. All Joseph ever took along with him was his prayer shawl and his staff. Jesus knew that his grandfather had taken Joseph along when he was about to come of age in the Jewish faith. Joseph's rich descriptions of his father and the time he spent with him had made him seem so real to Jesus that he felt as if he knew him. Soon he would be old enough to go along.

He smiled to himself, knowing that tomorrow would be a good day. Joseph never failed to return from his time away without having new and fresh insights into the scriptures that they would discuss while they worked.

Their days spent together working had a two-fold advantage. Joseph was able to use the concentrated time to teach Jesus the trade of carpentry and while they were working he taught him the ancient stories that affirmed the

Covenants that God had made with His chosen people.

And, at other times Jesus would ask his father if he could tell him one of the stories; Joseph always inspired by the fresh, exhilarating perspectives that Jesus found in them.

Jesus saw God as eternally benevolent, His mercy continually reaching around the ongoing betrayal of His people toward a time when God would reconcile them back to Himself. He saw God's love reaching out to all people through His people, the Jews.

They spent long hours together, big hands guiding little hands, creating practical items from the miracles that grew from the smallest seeds or nuts. Every time they took a tree to use, they prayed while bringing it back to the workshop, thanking God for the miracle of wood and of what they could create with it. Nothing was wasted; even the smallest scraps were used for fuel.

Joseph taught Jesus about stewardship, and how God had told Adam he was responsible to tend the world God had recreated for him. He described the two trees that God put in the center of the garden called "Eden"; the garden the Creator God had planted for Adam, and what those two trees represented in the story of mankind and his lost fellowship with God. Joseph explained that had Adam chosen to eat from the "tree of life" instead of from "the tree of the knowledge of good and evil" the result would have been that man would have remained in fellowship with their creator, but because he ate of the other tree, man and nature were both under a curse

Because of his father's reputation for compassion and generosity, there were people who contrived ways to pay him less than his hours of labor were worth. Joseph simply turned those matters over to God, never speaking of them again, believing that by doing so his reward was in walking in God's favor.

He was often the first to appear at their doorstep when there was a problem or a tragedy and it was just as likely that he would be the last to leave. He never turned away when he saw a need. If something was ever missing from their household Jesus knew without asking that it was likely that Joseph had offered it to someone to ease their discomfort. Poor or rich, gentile or Jew, if his papa saw a need he considered it an honor to be of assistance.

Oh, how Jesus loved him; the sweet smell of wood in his clothes and his beard was like perfume to him. He memorized every detail of Joseph's hands; he knew by heart every scar and callous that distinguished their years of hard work.

People who knew Joseph trusted him, often coming to him for counsel. Joseph willingly shared his precious time helping fix the intangible, also. He offered thanks for every person who crossed his doorstep, undertaking to do his very best in whatever he was asked to do. Whether the job was large or small, when Joseph finally delivered it, he delivered his blessing with it as well. Everyone was the same to Joseph. He had no need to impress anyone.

By example Joseph showed him that true wisdom came from waiting on God, and it was in those quiet moments the father and son shared something profound; a communion of spirit and a vision for a day when God would pour out His Spirit on His chosen ones who longed to know His voice.

Jesus lay on his pallet in the dark, listening to the sounds of his sleeping siblings. He joined his father in spirit, imagining him kneeling under a canopy of stars.

Jesus woke to the sounds of his father returning home just before dawn. Whatever it was that compelled Joseph to go into the hills rather than sleep, or to miss supper, he knew that Joseph had received what he sought from the Lord, and he wanted to know what that was like. Today would be special, for his papa's spirit would be overflowing from what he had received while waiting on God, alone under the night sky.

Today would be a thoughtful day, recalling God's promises and His covenants to His people. Jesus never tired of his father recalling the history of the Jewish people, and how God rescued them over and over again.

Yes, today was going to be a rich day.

CHAPTER ELEVEN

Joseph lingered behind so that he could watch Jesus play with his dog. It gave him pleasure to watch them chasing each other, both of them playful and full of youthful energy. This morning was no exception.

Jesus was a serious boy, and these rare moments of spontaneous frolicking were a gift for Joseph. It concerned him that his son's life was by necessity so solitary, but every moment must be seized. Time, for Joseph, had taken on a new dimension.

Jesus ran on ahead, racing toward their home. In the morning he and Joseph would be leaving with some other local tradesmen on a trip that would take them away for several days, having been commissioned to make the furnishings for a synagogue in another village. Jesus was excited to have been asked to accompany his father.

Joseph turned aside to secure the provisions they would need to take with them. Jesus headed home to double check their cargo; all meticulously laid out and ready to be packed for the trip.

When he approached the courtyard he could hear the sounds of objects being hurled against the walls of the workshop. His dog ran ahead, growling and the fur on her neck ruffled. Jesus ran toward the commotion; braced for the worst.

With dismay, he saw immediately that the workshop was in complete disarray. All of their work of the past few weeks had been undone; all of the organizing and inventorying of each separate piece, even their tools lay scattered across the floor.

His brother James stood in the midst of the chaos, his arm raised above his head prepared to hurl a hammer against the top piece of the *bimah* for the new synagogue. Sensing he was being watched, he turned defiantly toward his older brother.

Jesus said nothing but quietly moved inside, immediately bending over to begin the tedious task of restoring order to what had been carefully disassembled sections of furniture, that would be reassembled once delivered to the synagogue. He and Joseph had built each piece of furniture, fitting them together, and then disassembling them. Each separate piece had been numbered, so that once the pieces were transported by wagon to the location it would be a relatively simple task to put them back together again.

James glared at him with contempt, throwing the hammer defiantly against a beautiful piece of wood at Jesus's feet, leaving a gash where it hit.

Jesus wished there was a way to reach out to His brother, but it wasn't as though he hadn't tried. James resentment towards him was deep and some of it was understandable. He got to spend long days and nights with their father, and Jesus knew that James felt left out. James viewed Jesus as the obstacle to his being close to Joseph.

James hated him, and even more now watching Jesus wordlessly began to tidy up the mess that James had made. Jesus not only stole his father's attention, but he was praised for what they did together. James was blinded by jealousy.

Just once he would like to be able to punch it out and see who would win. He would win; he was sure of it. His brother was weak; he never stood up for himself.

He waited for some recrimination, and when none came he shoved Jesus aside before making his exit, hoping he could provoke him to fight back. Watching Jesus accept his vandalism with no comment robbed him of any of the satisfaction he felt for trying to upstage him. Once, just once …

In his haste to leave, James failed to notice his father, who stood out of sight around the corner of the house. Joseph had also heard the racket originating from within the workshop and had followed Jesus.

His was heavyhearted whenever he thought of the effect his time with Jesus had on James. *Oh, God, forgive me, but I am but one man!*

Joseph thought of another Joseph, the son of Jacob, and he believed that whatever pit one of God's chosen was placed in that God would use it for good if the one who suffered would look to Him for help. He believed that one day James would choose to give his anger to God, believing that God had a plan for him and would use him for His purposes. In the end, nothing would be wasted because God would take all of it and use it to glorify Himself.

Joseph turned his attention to the son who was trying to bring order out of the chaos of their carefully arranged project. Unaware of his father's presence, Jesus was focused on trying to undo as much of the damage as he could before his father returned. Joseph saw the streaks on his face that resulted from his sorrow at being rejected by his younger brother. Joseph marveled at the compassion Jesus could show even after receiving such undeserved treatment.

Joseph cleared his throat to give Jesus a moment to collect himself before he entered. When he walked into the courtyard he acted surprised by the disarray.

Jesus quickly wiped his eyes in his sleeve and stood up. All he said was, "I'm sorry, Papa."

He quickly turned away and continued the slow process of putting things back in order.

Joseph turned away from him also. The remarkable grace that was so natural to this young lad was beyond his ability to comprehend. He fought to control the tears that stung his own eyes. He bent over and joined Jesus in the unwelcome task of restoring their weeks of hard work, humbled by his son's gentle soul that often seemed so much older than his own

CHAPTER TWELVE

Joseph rose to his feet and walked to the front of the sanctuary, raising his *tallit* over his head, standing in front of the ark for a moment before opening it. He carefully removed one of the scrolls from inside. He brought it to his lips, kissing it before he placed it on the *bimah*.

He and his father had crafted the furniture in the synagogue. Together they had carved the symbols of their faith into the podium. His hand caressed the sacred altar, a silent tribute to his father's memory. A candle stand stood to his right offering barely enough light to read by, but that was of no concern to Joseph; he knew these scriptures by heart.

He nodded to the men assembled on the benches that lined both sides of the synagogue. It was the sundown on the Sabbath, and it was his turn to read from God's sacred scriptures.

"*Sh'ma Yisrael Adonai Eloheinu Adonai echad.*" "Hear, O Israel, the Lord your God the Lord is one."

Outside, Mary and Ruth waited for their husbands; waiting with their children and the other families whose husbands and sons were inside. Jesus stood next to her, deep in thought. He was concentrating; listening for when his father began his reading; hoping he could hear him.

Joseph unrolled the scroll and began reading from the book of Isaiah, 'Who has believed our message? To whom has the Lord revealed His powerful arm? My servant grew up in the Lord's presence like a tender green shoot, like a root in dry ground. There was nothing beautiful or majestic about His appearance, nothing to attract us to him. He was despised and rejected; a man of sorrows, acquainted with deepest grief. We turned our backs on Him and looked the other way. He was despised and we did not care. Yet it was our weaknesses He carried; it was our sorrows that weighed Him down. And we thought His troubles were a punishment from God, a punishment for His own sins! But He was pierced for our rebellion, crushed for our sins. He was beaten so we could be whole. He was whipped so we could be healed. All of us, like sheep, have strayed away.'

Joseph raised his eyes and looked toward the entrance to the synagogue; knowing that his family would be waiting for him there. The words from the prophet Isaiah had an unexpected impact on him; the words stuck in his throat. With shaking hands he unrolled the scroll to expose the remainder of the passage. He continued, 'He was oppressed and treated harshly...'

He cleared his throat, His voice hoarse. He tried to continue the reading but the words felt like knives piercing into His soul. Barely audible, he whispered, "...yet He never said a word. He was led like a lamb to the slaughter. And as a sheep is silent before the shearers, He did not open His mouth. Unjustly condemned He was led away. No one cared that he died without descendants, that His life was cut short in midstream. But He was struck down for the rebellion of my people. He had done no wrong and had never deceived anyone. But He was buried like a criminal; He was put in a rich man's grave. But, it was the Lord's good plan to crush Him and cause Him grief."

He swayed, grabbing onto the *bimah* for support. He fought off the sensation that he was going to be sick, moving cautiously around to the front of the podium and toward the door.

He walked off doing the unthinkable; he had left the scroll lying open.

Every eye was focused on him; he could hear the men murmuring to each other.

By now he was sweating and very cold. With relief he found himself standing outside the synagogue; he had no memory of how he got there.

Mary rushed to him, but Joseph walked right past her, through the small gathering, and toward their home like someone in a trance. What took place that Sabbath night was never mentioned again by either of them, but Mary saw in him a sadness that she had not seen before.

She couldn't bring herself to ask him why, because she wasn't ready to think about what lie ahead.

CHAPTER THIRTEEN

I t was a cold, starry night when Joseph and Jesus made their way up into the hills outside Nazareth.

The father walked in silence; his habit when he was listening for a word from the Lord. It was vital he be certain what God wanted of him, especially now. He and the boy were both waiting on God; asking Him to speak into their spirits His confirmation of what they both were feeling.

They sought answers to the many questions now stirring relentlessly inside them. Many of the questions were unspoken because they required answers that were unthinkable; perhaps because they already knew what the answers were.

Joseph's constant companion was a sense of melancholy, with each day marking time toward when his presence would no longer be a necessity in Jesus's life. He accepted that it was by sovereign design that he must step aside once Jesus took upon himself full ownership of the mantle being draped upon Him

It was time for Jesus to be told all of the events surrounding his birth and early childhood. Rumors still circulated; speculations about his and Mary's marriage and the years they were in Egypt. He knew that God would give them the right words to convey to Jesus who he was.

In some ways it seemed to him like it had happened so very long ago; that night when he woke from the dream that had catapulted him into his role of adopted father to a boy of unfathomable destiny. Yet, in reality the time had been short.

There had never been any distinction in Joseph's heart or his head between Jesus or his other children, other than the ever present and humbling awareness that Almighty God had chosen him to raise His son and equip him for the role he would play in man's redemption. *How was it possible for him to have functioned within that role?* Looking back, he wondered how he had been able to do any of it competently.

Nor had the dream had never lost its immediate impact, or any of its spiritual virility. All Joseph had to do was to meditate on God's word to have it reconfirmed to him again, leaving him no doubt, but a numbing knowing that God was about to do the extraordinary; to visit His people as one of them.

Joseph had never been able to see himself as part of Jesus' future as a man. With that urgency prompting him, he more and more insisted that Jesus relate back to him his revelations from the scriptures, hearing the words spoken through the boy as if he were one with them.

During those times of intimate fellowship Joseph would close his eyes and rest against the courtyard wall; listening to his son's soft voice reciting the familiar passages that he infused with the overlying truths that would mysteriously play themselves out through him in the years to come. Yes, the great I AM had put His own nature into flesh and blood born of Mary, and was about to do the unthinkable.

Joseph shook his head at the thought of how God was preparing to expose Himself with such imponderable vulnerability to a world that seemed so unprepared for what He was about to do.

The last Passover left Joseph with no remaining doubt that Jesus had embraced his calling, or his identification with the sacrifices that would accompany it. He now knew with certainty that he had transmitted into him what the scriptures taught about the one that God would send who, because he was sinless, could satisfy the penalty for sin … once; for all.

After they had arrived in Jerusalem for Passover Jesus went with Joseph to purchase their Paschal lamb. As was the custom, they brought it back with them to the camp for a prescribed time before the Passover sacrifice. It was a bittersweet time, watching the young animal nuzzling the children, accepting their demonstrations of tenderness when it became the family pet while they were waiting for the Day of Sacrifice to arrive. Even Joseph could not help but to smile at the lamb's comedic romping with the children.

The Day of Sacrifice dawned. It was only because of the lamb's blood that each family applied above and on each side of their doorposts that the Israelites firstborn were spared from the angel of death that would demand the firstborn children of the Egyptians.

The blood of the lamb would be their protection from the last plague pronounced over the Egyptians; the blood was their covering, and when they stepped outside through their doorways the next morning they would be forever marked as a people set apart for the Glory of God. And, now, thousands of years later, Jewish people still gathered to recall how God had birthed their nation, bringing them out of their slavery, first through the blood and then through the water.

Jesus had by now memorized the Torah and the books of the prophets. That was his rite of passage into Jewish manhood. This spring, for the first time he would go with his father to the

Temple to offer their family's lamb; a moving experience both for a father and his son.

It was time.

Joseph caught up the small creature that immediately began to bleat. Joseph held him close against his chest for a few moments to quiet him. He offered the now calm animal to Jesus, who reluctantly received the offering, conscious of the cost placed on this precious animal, now resting in his embrace. Suddenly the weight of the little lamb became almost unbearable.

In silence, the father and son made their way across the Hebron Valley, walking past the ancient olive garden where they would go to pray tonight after their Passover meal, then they crossed the Hebron River, passed through the Eastern Gate, moving ever upwards toward the temple, its breathtaking dimensions looming ahead.

Many fathers and sons crossed over the valley along with them, a few sang psalms, but most were silent, the quietness of the procession speaking loudly to the solemnity of the moment.

Abruptly, the stillness was broken by the racket of the merchants and money changers, greedy to line their pockets using the pilgrim's yearly visit to Jerusalem to sell their wares. The lines were long; those who had arrived late were waiting impatiently to purchase their lambs. A cold brisk wind whipped through the passages. Jesus shuddered, his spirit recoiling at the lack of respect shown to this place where God had said He wanted to meet with His people.

Joseph put his hand on his son's shoulder, guiding him through the mayhem toward the Temple, now looming over them. He knew his son was disquieted by the commotion going on around them.

Protectively, his fingers tightened.

It was their turn.

They stepped forward, Jesus still clutching the baby lamb.

The Priest was sensitive to the young man's reluctant release of the lamb, having many times seen the shock the sacrifice was to the young men who were presenting their lambs for the first time and dealing with the reality of atonement. He took the animal from Jesus, laying it on its side on the slab in front of them. The lamb lay there quietly and did not struggle, its eyes fixed on Jesus who tenderly reached out to touch the little head one last time.

As the priest intoned the ageless words of the *Hallel* over the offering, Jesus moved sideways toward and into his father.

Joseph absorbed into himself his son's trembling, firmly drawing him close, remembering the first time he had stood by his father and could comprehend the reality of the cost of his own sin. He knew this day would be significant for them both in a dimension far beyond what anyone else had ever known, or would be asked to know.

The knife was raised, and as quickly as the priest brought the blade down, severing the artery in the neck of the baby animal, its coal black eyes stared unblinking back at them. The lamb's life was in its blood, and while the blood was carefully and reverently collected, Jesus recognized God's grace in His provision for man's sin in the sacrificial act of mercy that required the innocent life.

Jesus stared at the now bloodless sacrifice. He now knew why the lamb had seemed so heavy, for a weight had been transferred into his spirit along with a knowing too terrible for words…

He was the lamb.

CHAPTER FOURTEEN

J oseph studied his son. This moment was what he had been preparing him for from the beginning. He had never held back, but had taught him what the scriptures taught about the promised Messiah. What was required was hard; harsh … it had to be. Man's redemption hung on the innocent sacrifice that God would offer for mankind to atone for man's sin once and for all.

The fact that he was standing on Mt. Moriah washed over him. This was where God had first revealed himself to Abraham as Jehovah Jirah; the God of Provision.

God had required that Abraham sacrifice his son, Isaac; the child of promise. Abraham had brought him here in total obedience; he had climbed the same slope, heavy hearted with dread, but convinced that what Jehovah asked of him could not be withheld; convinced that Jehovah could raise Isaac from the dead once the sacrifice was met.

Isaac had willingly carried the wood that would be used for the sacrifice. Abraham had assured the servants they would return after they worshipped the Lord; Abraham convinced that God would not break Covenant with him; sacrifice and worship bonded into one act.

What words were exchanged between the father and son while they climbed to the summit? he wondered. *Or had they walked in silence?* Words were useless when trying to convey mysteries so deep.

Isaac would not have been a small child when Abraham brought him here; he would have been a young man, perhaps about twenty years old. Isaac had questioned his father about where the sacrifice they were to offer was.

Together they had determined that God's Will be carried out, trusting God with the details of how He would bring His Covenant to pass. They both knew that Isaac was the son who carried the promised seed.

What did Abraham say to help Isaac understand that he was the sacrifice? Whatever they said to each other, Isaac had willingly offered himself.

Joseph and his son watched the Priest catch the lamb's blood in a golden goblet and hand it to another priest who handed it to another until the blood was sprinkled on the altar; the blood was caught and passed in that fashion until it was completely drained from the animal.

The lamb was hung on hooks to be skinned, its fat was removed and burned on the altar, its organs removed and cleansed according to the instructions in the Talmud. Then, wrapped in a shroud of linen, the lamb was returned to them to be roasted and consumed that same night.

Joseph felt old. Again, his thoughts turned to Abraham; who would have stood near where he was now, the knife poised for the sacrifice, and then the awful silence broken, "Abraham! Abraham!" and his quick response, "Here I am!"

The angel of God spoke the words of reprieve to the father, "Don't lay a hand on the boy, for now I know that you truly fear God for you have not withheld from me your son, your only son."

Abraham turned and saw a ram caught by its horns in a thicket and offered it in place of his son. "On the mountain of the Lord it will be provided."

There could be no such reprieve for Jesus. Joseph knew the plan. A sinless substitute must take upon him the sins of all mankind. A redeemer would take the punishment for the lost family of man; God's provision for him as well. Joseph's eyes spilled over.

Soon, very soon, he would, must, be removed from the stage where the most profound drama in the history of man would soon be played out. He wondered if God would give him a sign.

Seconds before Abraham would have sacrificed his son God spoke to him through an angel, telling him to put down his knife; that there was a substitute. Joseph looked around; there would be no thicket, no ram, no reprieve ...

Oh, God, his heart cried. *How can you offer him, this perfect lamb?*

The lad standing next to him would willingly offer himself for that purpose; to receive into himself every sin, no matter how vile, how repulsive, how vulgar ... along with Joseph's own.

The processing of the lamb was finished. Joseph reached out to take the soggy parcel, but Jesus stepped in front of him. He put out his arms. The attendant handed him the lamb; lighter in mass, but incalculably heavier in reality. Its little head lolled to the side, exposing the gaping gash where the knife had struck. Joseph reached out to catch its little head in his hand. He adjusted the linen wrapped lamb so that it rested firmly against Jesus's chest.

In silence the father and son walked out of the Temple, back through the chaotic din of the vendors, and across the valley to their waiting family. Below them the stream had turned bright red from the overflow of the sacrifices still being offered high above them.

Tonight they would celebrate the Passover; when the blood of the lamb had held at bay the angel of judgment and death.

Joseph sighed; he was very tired.

Something told him this would be the last time he would return to Jerusalem.

EPILOGUE

Jesus was out of breath, having run most of the way home. He pushed through the cluster of relatives and neighbors who had gathered outside his parent's home, acknowledging their condolences before going inside. Although he would have preferred more privacy, he recognized their affection for Joseph and the need to be together while they waited for the news they did not want to hear.

He entered the house and walked straight into the arms of his mother who was waiting for him by the opening to her and Joseph's sleeping alcove. She had been waiting for him to arrive having sent for him knowing that Joseph's time was at hand.

Her eyes searched the eyes of her son, drawing strength from them. Jesus's solemn calmness helped her momentarily not despair for the loneliness that she knew would soon own her. There were no words…

Joseph had been preparing her for this moment from the time they had found their lost son in the temple after Passover the spring before. He had returned to Nazareth a changed man. Quietly he put his and Mary's life in order.

He spoke words of peace and comfort to his wife, trying to prepare her for what had become obvious to him. While he sorted through the details of what he hoped would make her life easier when she was alone, in the end he had to once again abandon himself to his Lord. All he could do was again trust in God to complete the work he had begun, but knowing he must leave her almost broke his heart.

Once again, Joseph had found peace in his own obedience to his task. He had not turned to the right or to the left: he had used every possible moment to mentor his son and care for his family. God had blessed him far beyond anything he might have imagined.

Joseph knew that he had completed the assignment that God had given him that night so long ago. Once again, God had given him his sign; he had known from the moment they had found Jesus in the Temple that his part of Jesus's journey had ended.

Mary wasn't ready, but she had also accepted this as part of God's plan for her; having known that their journey had been designed by a higher order and required far more than what she or Joseph could fully comprehend.

Jesus slipped past her into the alcove, looking down to where Joseph was resting propped up on cushions to help him to breathe. Joseph opened his eyes, his hand rising from off the pallet in acknowledgment of his son's arrival, having already sensed that he was near. In the end, what they had to say to each other had been transmitted in the language of profound silences.

In the wall across from where Joseph was lying was a small window, covered by a curtain. Jesus reached up and pulled it aside, allowing light and fresh air into the dark room. "Abba, now you can see the sky." Joseph smiled as he looked upward toward the sky, a tear slipping down his cheek. Together they had spent countless hours looking into the heavens. God was big. Jesus wanted his father to think on that. The little window once again cast its light over Joseph.

Jesus knelt on the floor beside his father. He picked up Joseph's hand; it was cold. He turned it over slowly and thoughtfully, looking over the familiar hand that had been there from His birth until today; that had been placed on him for blessing throughout his life and had shown Him by example the honor of hard work. Jesus kissed it and held it to his cheek. How he would miss this lovely, quiet man.

Joseph had done his job well. Jesus' young spirit had grown strong and capable because of his tutoring and example. Jesus had embraced his mission and understood the sacrifices that would accompany it.

Because of Joseph's example, he had experienced the value of time spent alone seeking God and waiting for Him to speak. Together they had celebrated the voice that had so often come to them in those seasons of waiting, confirming the scriptures to them.

Joseph's tender devotion to Mary was a precious legacy; to have observed the value that Joseph placed on his wife as an equal. It blessed him to think of Joseph's love and respect for his mother as his helper in life, never dismissing her, but cherishing her observations and opinions.

From the beginning of his earthly life, Jesus had been wrapped in the unconditional love of a father who had put his family before himself, selflessly attempting to meet each need, and giving God his inadequacies when he couldn't. He accepted what little he received in return like priceless treasure.

Joseph's faith in the unseen had beamed its light across the shadows of the life God had chosen for him instead. Nobility disguised as a tradesman, known as "the carpenter" to the people who depended on him.

Joseph motioned toward a corner of the room, where his prayer shawl had been carefully placed over some objects. Jesus stood up. He gently removed the *tallit* and unfolded it. He grasped the beloved garment of his father to his heart before placing it over his head, turning to his father. Joseph nodded his approval as he did so. This simple mantle embodied the promises of God and the generations of Jewish fathers who taught their sons the Torah and reverence for God's calling to His special people. Henceforth, it would call to his remembrance the love of his earthly father.

Beneath it was a seamless linen robe, carefully folded and resting on top of several ornate boxes. These were the gifts from the wise men, diligently guarded by Joseph over the years and now given to the one sought by the magi that starry night in Bethlehem. Jesus' eyes brimmed with tears, knowing his father could have used the wealth in those boxes on many occasions when he and Mary found themselves wondering how they would get by. Now, as Joseph was about to leave them, he was entrusting Jesus with the provision God had given in the beginning for Jesus' and Mary's life without him.

With effort, Joseph opened his eyes to look one last time upon the face of the young man whose destiny it would be to redeem mankind and bring him back into fellowship with God. He had always known his influence was by necessity temporary so that Jesus would identify completely with the Eternal Father. Joseph had no regrets; his life had been willingly offered, even now. He motioned for Jesus to bend close to him. "I want to bless you, my son," he whispered.

Jesus bent low over his father; feeling his father's hand rest heavily on his head. He lowered his head so his ear was close to Joseph's mouth, ensuring he would not miss even one of the words he would cherish through eternity.

This would be the last blessing he would receive from his earthly father, whose companionship had led him into fellowship with God, and into his purpose for being here. He received the whispered blessing into his spirit, drawing strength from Joseph's unwavering faith in the eternal God. He stood up and beckoned to his brothers and sisters to one by one come into the alcove so Joseph could bless each of them, knowing they each longed for one last word from their beloved father. After the blessings were spoken he left the room so that Mary and Joseph could have time alone.

The hours passed slowly, with Jesus sitting beside Joseph's pallet. He reflected on the rich legacy imparted into him through this man. He watched Joseph's chest slowly rise and fall, each breath becoming more labored than the last.

Jesus refused to leave Joseph's side, even for a moment, so as not to be absent for the moment his father would leave them. He broke the silence only to offer thanks or sing the psalms of David over his father.

Mother and son maintained their vigil beside him as the sky grew dark and the stars could be seen twinkling through the small window in the wall above them, the only light a flickering oil lamp in a niche on the wall. Mary leaned against Jesus, her hand resting on Joseph's arm, her head on the shoulder of her son. Jesus held Joseph's hand.

They did not weep, although that time would come. Words for the moment had become meaningless, swallowed up in the shared, sweet reflections of the life of the man who had been integral to their own missions from Jehovah, Joseph's part of their journey now completed.

As Joseph's earthly life was ebbing away Jesus bent forward and again put his cheek against his father's. He whispered softly into his father's ear the words of Job: "For I know that my Redeemer lives, and that he shall stand at the latter day upon the earth: and though worms destroy this body, yet in my flesh shall I see God."

He squeezed Joseph's hand, assuring him, "He has come, Papa. The Redeemer has come."

Joseph's eyes fluttered, and with a sigh, he released his spirit into eternity, anonymous to but a few.

The plan intended to reconcile fallen mankind back to the Father, the plan conceived before the foundation of the world had begun, and no force would be able to stop it.

A father had been chosen before time began; chosen, if you will, by the very son of the Most High God whom he would raise.

Joseph entered eternity having fulfilled a calling history was forbidden to put into words, his silent legacy profoundly mirrored by the Son of God and man who came to bring heaven's light to a darkened world: our world.

The light came, and the darkness could not extinguish it. It shines now, even brighter because of the darkness. That light who is the Living Word became human *like we are* and dwelt among us.

Jesus had a daddy, and his name was Joseph.

"Well done, good and faithful servant."

Post Script

Joseph of Nazareth is mentioned but a few times in the scriptures. We are introduced to him when he and Mary are betrothed, in the dream where he is told that Mary's child was from the Holy Spirit, and again when he and Mary travel to Bethlehem and when their baby is born.

We find him with his family at the Temple when Jesus was eight days old, another time when he is warned in a dream to flee to Egypt, and again when an angel tells him in a dream it is safe to return home. The last time we see him is when he and Mary searched for him and find him in the Temple. Four thousand three hundred and eighty days are reflected in the twelve years of their parenting to that time.

Profound details, hidden like buried treasure between the lines; the missing pieces of a puzzle. And, if you look closely at the Son you will see attributes of character that were shaped in part, by the influences that were modeled throughout his life in the institution that God birthed in Eden; where a mother and a father fulfill the roles that together are the basis for the family.

There are treasures hidden within the scriptures, and it is the Father's delight when His children will slow down, sit at His feet, and ask Him to tell His story to them.

Don't you love that God allowed Joseph to be present in the Temple when Jesus debated the religious leaders and then was reminded by Jesus that they should have looked for him there in the first place? I have to believe that along with the obvious relief he felt when they found him was also a tremendous satisfaction to see Jesus handily scoring points with the Jewish leadership.

The scriptures tell us Jesus was twelve years old at that time. That age marks a significant passage for a young Jewish boy, because spiritually he is considered a man. The story of Jesus in the Temple tells us that Jesus's knowledge of the Pentateuch and the writings of the prophets astonished the eldership of the Temple. Considering the obscurity of his upbringing, his knowledge of the word and the insights he shared that day put him at an unusual level of both comprehension and communication, as well as a remarkable sense of self–esteem to be so confident in that position.

In the time of Jesus, it would have been the father who was commanded by the law to "teach his children the ways of the Lord" and to "call to remembrance His mighty acts in behalf of His people". It was the father's responsibility to see that the next generation was baptized into their spiritual heritage.

Rule after rule had been added to the Law, obscuring the delight of serving and loving God by living within it to an overwhelming despair at the possibility of how to keep it. Within those formulas of strict observance a natural by-product would have been for the Jewish people to see God as equally strict while the corrupted

Priesthood used their fear of God for their own personal gain. Might that still be said of *religion* today?

Throughout the Bible there has always been a remnant who could see around the Law as a burdensome set of rules and instead sought the heart of Jehovah; the same remnant bringing joy to the God who has been reaching out to them through time and space to have relationship with man based on mutuality. The promises of God throughout scripture belong to those people. The promises are for those of us who share that longing and are called *Abraham's seed;* the just living by faith. Joseph was able to see far beyond his own time and space, having a heart tuned to knowing God in His Word; and, in truth, abiding in it. And because God could trust him to act with immediacy, he was entrusted with the responsibility to raise His son. We can only touch the surface of what that kind of faith and obedience means to the heart of the Father.

Somewhere inside eternity God set apart two people from David's ancestry. Both Mary and Joseph were from that lineage.

One day in the future the One the earth has groaned for will come again to earth.

The Heavenly Bridegroom will set His feet upon the Mount of Olives, returning the way He departed. He will bring with Him the Church; His Bride, the redeemed saints who chose Him as Lord, esteeming Him above everything else.

They will be joined by a brotherhood of Jews who at last recognize Him as their Messiah; their wilderness journey at last behind them.

The Champion of Champions returned to earth; the conquering hero who will govern with Truth. Justice and Fairness; the new rule of law that will issue forth from the One who was judged, condemned, and received no mercy.

Picture Him, our Heavenly Prince, walking down the path He took on Palm Sunday: past the Garden where He consented to the Father's will; betrayed into the hands of His executioners with a kiss.

Nature itself is released to celebrate and spontaneously offers its praise to the life–giver. The abundance intended in the beginning springs to life as He makes His way to the Holy City.

The curse reversed and Eden regained; the serpent's head crushed by the One he killed but could not keep; the deliberately corrupted creator, the lamb slain before the foundation of the world, sacrificed once … for all.

Jesus, Name above all Names, swinging from His fingertips the keys of death and hell. The Eastern Gate bursts open to receive Jerusalem's long–promised King. ….

The streets fill to overflowing with the rejoicing throng … as far as the eye can see, those who have been purchased for the Father by the

Son lift their hands to honor Him, shouting, "Hosanna in the Highest."

Try to imagine the deafening swell that fills the air; of songs, and shouting, and laughing; the cheering, the clapping..."*Hallelujah! Hallelujah! Hallelujah!*"

He makes His way to the Temple, the High Priest of Heaven, whose sacrifice has been accepted by the Father. The Holy of Holies forever opened wide...

The Risen Redeemer climbs the steps of the Temple to take His Throne; the Anointed One to be anointed again, this time as King. He will rule the earth from David's throne, in David's city, complete with David bowing before the One whose heart he blessed.

A couple leans against the stone wall in the Temple courtyard.

He reaches out for her hand, taking it into his. Together they take in the spectacle now unfolding all around them ...

She looks up at him. Her eyes are radiant. He looks at her and smiles. He can read her thoughts, for they are his own.

This is their moment of truth. Everything they were asked to sacrifice, everything they counted as nothing to be obedient to the will of the Father, everything they had offered to Him was a small price for the exceeding great wonder of this moment ...

Their voices join the choruses of praise, singing,

For to us a child is born,
unto us a son is given,
and the government will be on his shoulders.
And he will be called
Wonderful Counselor,
Mighty God,
Everlasting Father,
Prince of Peace.

His reign will be forever! Amen!

END NOTES

Included are scriptures used to form the basis for the story.

Prologue
Scriptures pertaining to Joseph of Nazareth
Matthew 1: 16, 18, 19, 20, 24 Matthew 2: 13, 19,
Luke 1:27 Luke 2:4 Luke 2:16 Luke 2:33 Luke
2:43 Luke 3:23 Luke 4:22 John 1:45
Scriptures pertaining to Simeon and Anna
Luke 2: 21–36
Scripture pertaining to Jesus with the elders
Luke 2: 41–52

Chapter One
Psalm 119 Psalm 51 Duet. 32:10

Chapter Two
Matthew 1:18–25 Luke 1: 26–28 Luke 1: 39–56
Duet. 22: 23,24 Jeremiah 1:12

Chapter Three
Scriptures pertaining to Zechariah and Elizabeth: Luke 1: 5–25 Luke 1: 65–66

Chapter Four
Scriptures pertaining to the wise men: Psalm 72:
10, 11, 15 Micah 5:2 Matthew 2: 1–11
Scriptures pertaining to slaughter of male children in Bethlehem and flight into Egypt: Jeremiah 31: 15 Matthew 2: 13–23:

Chapter Six
Scriptures pertaining to Joseph's return from exile with his family: Hosea 11:1 Matthew 2:15

Chapter Seven
Psalm 23
Isaiah 51:3
Psalm 121

Chapter nine
Genesis 2

Chapter twelve
Duet. 6: 4–9
Isaiah 53

Chapter thirteen
Exodus chapter 12

The blood from the Paschal lamb was first sprinkled on the door-posts of the Israelites in Egypt. It was to be a sign to the 'angel of death' to 'pass over' the houses of the Israelites when passing through the land to slay the Egyptians first born children. This sacrifice called the "Mishnah", or "Pesah Mizrayim". God's instructions to Moses were for His Covenant people to observe this annually for all times after entering the Promised land. (Exodus 12:25) The Passover given to succeeding generations is called the "Pesah Dorot".

Numbers 9:1–3: (NLT) A year after Israel's departure from Egypt, the Lord spoke to Moses in the wilderness of Sinai. In the first month of that year (the month of Nissi on the Jewish calendar) he said, "Tell the Israelites to celebrate the Passover at the prescribed time, at twilight of the fourteenth day of the first month. Be sure to follow all my decrees and regulations concerning this celebration."

The Paschal sacrifice was discontinued after the Temple was destroyed in 70 AD The Seder of today includes the roasted shankbone of a lamb.

It is the hope of the Orthodox Jew that another Temple will be built in Jerusalem, and there is preparation for that day currently taking place by the assembling of items necessary for it to be reinstituted. On that day they again will sacrifice the Paschal lamb.

As Christians, we believe that Jesus fulfilled the requirements of the Law and that by His sacrifice atonement was for sin was made, once and for all, who believe on His name.

Chapter Fourteen

Genesis 22

Approximately twenty major references are found in the New Testament relating to the return of Christ: Matt 19:28; 23:39 ; 24:3—25:46

Mark 13:24–37

Luke 12:35–48; 17:22–37 ; 18:8 ; 21:25–28

Acts 1:10–11; 15:16–18

Rom 11:25–27

1 Cor 11:26

2 Thess 1:7–10; 2:8

2 Pet 3:3–4

Jude 1:14–15

Rev 1:7–8; 2:25–28; 16:15 ; 19:11–21 ; 22:20

Old Testament scriptures which likewise describe deliverance that will take place at the time of the second advent:

Zech 14:1–4).

The Scriptures also tell us that at the second coming Israel will experience spiritual revival. Romans 11:26–27 implies this, and also Jeremiah 31.

Amos 9:11–12

Ezekiel 37:24 speaks of Israel's regathering.

Ezekiel 37:26: "He shall be great, and shall be called the Son of the Most High: and the Lord God shall give unto him the throne of his father David: and he shall reign over the house of Jacob for ever; and of his kingdom there shall be no end."

Definitions:

Tallit: (Hebrew: טַלִית) a Jewish prayer shawl

Bimah: (or tebah) is the elevated area or platform in a Jewish Synagogue which is intended to serve the place where the person reading aloud from the Torah stands during the part of the service where the Torah is read.

listen|imagine|view|experience

AUDIO BOOK DOWNLOAD INCLUDED WITH THIS BOOK!

In your hands you hold a complete digital entertainment package. In addition to the paper version, you receive a free download of the audio version of this book. Simply use the code listed below when visiting our website. Once downloaded to your computer, you can listen to the book through your computer's speakers, burn it to an audio CD or save the file to your portable music device (such as Apple's popular iPod) and listen on the go!

How to get your free audio book digital download:

1. Visit www.tatepublishing.com and click on the e|LIVE logo on the home page.
2. Enter the following coupon code:
   41ec-146e-d5cc-f8dc-c0d0-b69d-5a0a-1ab1
3. Download the audio book from your e|LIVE digital locker and begin enjoying your new digital entertainment package today!